Sword Art: Online Alternative
Gun Gale

X

5th Squad Ja

Keiichi Sigsawa

ILLUSTRATION BY
Kouhaku Kuroboshi

SUPERVISED BY
Reki Kawahara

CONTENTS

DESIGN: BEE-PEE

Sword Art Online Alternative

GUN GALE ONLINE

XII

5th Squad Jam:
Continue

Keiichi Sigsawa

ILLUSTRATION BY
Kouhaku Kuroboshi

SUPERVISED BY
Reki Kawahara

YEN
ON

NEW YORK

SWORD ART ONLINE Alternative Gun Gale Online, Vol. 12
KEIICHI SIGSAWA

Translation by Stephen Paul
Cover art by Kouhaku Kuroboshi

SWORD ART ONLINE Alternative Gun Gale Online Vol. XII
©Keiichi Sigsawa, Reki Kawahara 2021
Edited by Dengeki Bunko
First published in Japan in 2022 by KADOKAWA CORPORATION, Tokyo.
English translation rights arranged with KADOKAWA CORPORATION, Tokyo, through TUTTLE-MORI AGENCY, INC., Tokyo.

English translation © 2023 by Yen Press, LLC

Yen On
150 West 30th Street, 19th Floor
New York, NY 10001

Visit us at yenpress.com * facebook.com/yenpress * twitter.com/yenpress * yenpress.tumblr.com * instagram.com/yenpress

First Yen On Edition: June 2023
Edited by Yen On Editorial: Payton Campbell
Designed by Yen Press Design: Andy Swist

Yen On is an imprint of Yen Press, LLC.
The Yen On name and logo are trademarks of Yen Press, LLC.

Library of Congress Cataloging-in-Publication Data
Names: Sigsawa, Keiichi, 1972– author. | Kuroboshi, Kouhaku, illustrator. |
    Kawahara, Reki, supervisor. | Paul, Stephen (Translator), translator.
Title: Fifth Squad Jam: Start / Keiichi Sigsawa ; illustration by Kouhaku Kuroboshi ; supervised by
    Reki Kawahara ; translation by Stephen Paul ; cover art by Kouhaku Kuroboshi.
Description: First Yen On edition. | New York : Yen On, 2018– |
    Series: Sword art online alternative gun gale online ; Volume 12
Identifiers: LCCN 2018009303 | ISBN 9781975327521 (v. 1 : pbk.) |
    ISBN 9781975353841 (v. 2 : pbk.) | ISBN 9781975353858 (v. 3 : pbk.) |
    ISBN 9781975353865 (v. 4 : pbk.) | ISBN 9781975353872 (v. 5 : pbk.) |
    ISBN 9781975353889 (v. 6 : pbk.) | ISBN 9781975315320 (v. 7 : pbk.) |
    ISBN 9781975315979 (v. 8 : pbk.) | ISBN 9781975315993 (v. 9 : pbk.) |
    ISBN 9781975321802 (v. 10 : pbk.) | ISBN 9781975348564 (v. 11 : pbk.) |
    ISBN 9781975367862 (v. 12 : pbk.)
Subjects: | CYAC: Fantasy games—Fiction. | Virtual reality—Fiction. | Role playing—Fiction. |
    BISAC: FICTION / Science Fiction / Adventure.
Classification: LCC PZ7.1.S537 Sq 2018 | DDC [Fic]—dc23
LC record available at https://lccn.loc.gov/2018009303

ISBNs: 978-1-9753-6786-2 (paperback)
    978-1-9753-6787-9 (ebook)

10 9 8 7 6 5 4 3 2 1

LSC-C

Printed in the United States of America

Sword Art Online Alternative
GUN GALE ONLINE

Playback
of
5th SQUAD JAM

SYNOPSIS OF PART I

Less than a month after SJ4, *GGO*'s premiere team battle-royale event, Squad Jam, announced a fifth competition: SJ5. Once again, the sponsor was that terrible writer. He never learns.

This time for sure, Llenn thought, she would be able to just enjoy the game for the sake of it, with no weird pressure or annoying limitations. And yet again, she was disappointed.

Someone had put down a stunning bounty of a hundred million *GGO* credits, meaning one million actual real-life yen, on her head. In other words, everyone would be gunning for her, trying to get that cash.

Thanks to that, even her teammates were tempted to go after her. What a wonderful predicament to be in...

...But Llenn didn't give up.

Buoyed by a promise of cooperation from the furious SHINC, Llenn entered the event with her usual teammates of Pitohui, M, and Fukaziroh—plus Shirley, who would act independently and attack Pitohui whenever she felt like it, and her faithful companion (?) Clarence—hoping to secure her third win.

This time there was a special set of rules that permitted each player to carry a full separate set of equipment for a teammate and to switch between loadouts. So everyone picked out something a little different this time. Llenn's and Fukaziroh's choices were still a mystery.

And then SJ5 began.

Apparently determined to live up to his horrendous reputation, the crappy writer set up even more ridiculous rules.

Right at the start of the game, all the members of the team were scattered across the map.

And the battle arena was covered in thick fog that only revealed a space a few yards around each player. Llenn was all alone in a world she could barely see. How lonely.

She was unable to use her comm or compass, and even the terrain she was looking at didn't show up on the map. How awful.

Despite this, Llenn proceeded through the mist in search of her teammates and her friends in SHINC. Hang in there, Llenn.

And then who should she run into by coincidence but the brilliant strategist who led ZEMAL to a crushing victory in SJ4: Vivi.

Rather than attempt to kill each other, Llenn and Vivi chose a temporary partnership. Under Vivi's instructions, they carefully survived the battles in the fog.

But after an enormous explosion from the familiar suicide-bomb-happy squad, Vivi was the unlucky one, nearly dying from the blast.

To Llenn's good fortune, just nearby and rushing over to assist was the pairing of Boss and David, who helped Vivi survive the incident.

Four players from different teams worked as a new squad, taking positions inside a large, sturdy brick house.

They were planning to wait out the clearing mist inside the safety of the house—when one of ZEMAL's members, Shinohara, came rushing toward the building.

Delighted that they'd have another friend to help out, Llenn could only watch in horror as Shinohara was shot and killed from behind by the grenadier he'd been working with just moments earlier.

Llenn knew of only one grenadier who would commit such cowardly acts without hesitation—and her bad feeling was promptly proven correct.

It was Fukaziroh.

Why the hell would you do that?

CHAPTER 6

Ten-Minute Massacre Again

SECT.6

CHAPTER 6
Ten-Minute Massacre Again

"Viiiviiii! You biiiiitch! Time to answer for yeeeears of your criiiiiimes!"

"Oh no," Llenn lamented, looking to the sky.

"This is a grudge maaaatch! A hundred years in the makiiiiing! I'm going to use my plasma grenades to blow that entire house off this plaaaaaaneeeeeeeeeet!"

It was Fukaziroh's voice.

It was her, after all.

Yes, I knew it was. I knew it was.

It was difficult to understand how Fukaziroh's tiny body could project such a booming voice.

"Are there any baaaad little Vivis in the hooouuuse?!"

What are you, a demon?! Llenn snapped to herself. The sudden burst of mental activity got her brain working again.

What do I do? How do I resolve this situation peacefully?

The answer was simple.

I can't.

With Fukaziroh here, there was no way the five of them could enjoy SJ5 together, giggling and laughing all the while. It was hopeless.

So into her comm she said, "Everyone, out of the building! Run!" to all of her *current* teammates: Vivi, Boss, and David.

Her command was nearly drowned out by the sound of grenades exploding against the house. The successive blasts rocked the walls of the building.

These were normal grenade rounds. They scattered shrapnel meant for soft targets in a radius of about ten feet. A tough brick building like this one wouldn't fall from a couple of these hits.

But plasma grenades were a different story.

"Fuka's got a dozen plasma grenades! Once she runs out of regular grenades, she'll reload and fire all she's got!"

They would create a blue plasma blast with a radius of ten yards—a diameter of twenty—that would destroy everything within its range. If she fired twelve of them all in a row, the upstairs of the house would be gone, along with the first floor. Only the foundation would be left.

Wherever Fukaziroh the big bad wolf was, she probably had a hazy view of the house through the mist. And with her Bombardment skill, she could easily blast a hazy target at this range.

The explosions continued to boom away. It was evidence that Fukaziroh was more than happy to empty out the six-shot capacity of her two MGL-140 launchers.

An MGL-140 twisted to move the revolving magazine, and it would take the same amount of time and trouble to expel an unused grenade as it would to expel the empty cartridge after shooting it. In fact, it would take *longer* to shoot them all out, but she was going ahead with it anyway. That was how Fukaziroh lived her life: manly. Er, womanly.

But because of that, it gave the people inside precious extra seconds to save their own skin.

"Exit to the west!" David shouted, seeing and understanding all.

He'd probably jumped out the window in his room. The better a player, the less hesitation they had when their lives were on the line. Instant, snap judgment.

"Llenn, what do we do?!" hissed Boss into Llenn's left ear. It was a simple question, but Llenn understood the implication.

Fukaziroh was Llenn's teammate, and Boss was assisting

LPFM. Ordinarily, there was something only Boss could do in this situation.

She would have to kill Vivi right away and escape to the east with Llenn so they could reunite with Fukaziroh. That would be the most favorable outcome.

In other words, Boss was asking, *Should I just kill Vivi? She's tough, and ZEMAL is bad news with her leading them. Considering what's likely to happen in SJ5, this might be the best possible outcome. It would be reeeal easy right now...*

Understanding her meaning perfectly, Llenn promptly replied, "Both of you, get away from the building right now! I'll go out the west side, too!"

"Got it! C'mon, Vivi!" Boss said, rushing the other woman.

Llenn exited her room into the hallway. She was moving west when she heard loud footsteps behind her, most likely from Boss and Vivi, but she couldn't turn around to check. If Vivi shot her in the back, she wouldn't see it coming.

But if she did, Boss would shoot Vivi next. Vivi wouldn't go down without a fight, though. She'd put up resistance, and the whole thing would turn into a chaotic melee.

If you shoot me, so be it, but please don't shoot if you can help it! Llenn prayed.

Ultimately, there was no shot. Llenn hurried into the west-facing room where Vivi had initially been, hurtling through the haggard bedroom.

She bounded over a crushed, rotten bed, leaping toward the broken window, and threw herself through it into open air.

GGO players had no qualms about jumping out of second-story windows, a drop of ten to twelve feet. She landed and did a forward roll, clutching her P90 to her chest. The fall did almost no damage. Everyone in the game did this all the time, to the point that you had to be careful you didn't get carried away and do it in real life.

Right as Llenn recovered from her roll, she saw that Vivi was still airborne. Boss was in the window behind her.

Please make it in time! Llenn prayed, and took off running, hoping to get as far from the house as she could.

She looked over her shoulder once she was about ten yards away and saw that Fukaziroh's rage was indeed being manifested upon the building.

"Oh no…"

Large blue spheres were blooming over the house—a bombardment of plasma grenades.

It was a Fukaziroh-like assault, very Fukaziroh-like, indeed. She unleashed a full twelve-spot of plasmas, her maximum firepower, with no thought for the lasting consequences.

The eerie, bulging blue shapes swallowed the large brick house, literally pulverizing it. Fukaziroh's aim was unerring. She was an incredible shot with those launchers, but this was no time to admire skills.

The amalgamation of bricks could not withstand the force of sci-fi plasma explosives. The bricks were crushed into dust, practically returning to the dirt.

Vivi and Boss sprinted as hard as their legs would allow in the foreground of this vision of destruction. The ever-composed Vivi was actually grimacing with desperation, and Boss's eyes were so wide they were white all around the edges, making her look like a slapstick comic book character.

Running for their lives paid off, because those lives were still intact, but it didn't protect them from the explosions' blast wind.

"Aaah!"

"Dwaa!"

They were buffeted from behind and hurtled straight toward Llenn.

"Eep!"

She had no time to dodge, so Vivi's and Boss's considerably larger bodies slammed into Llenn's.

"Hya!"

"Gwufh!"

"Eeeek!"

All three of them tumbled spectacularly through the dark soil in the yard of the mansion.

"Yeeesh…"

Llenn opened her eyes, having been turned into a human pancake. The only thing she saw was Boss's back, broad and flat like an aircraft carrier. Boss had landed facedown and was smooshing Llenn's lower half.

I sure am getting knocked over a lot today, Llenn thought, checking her health on the readout in the corner. She'd lost a small amount of HP.

She was now under 70 percent, so she decided to be smart and just go ahead and take the emergency med kit.

Llenn was just lifting her head with her plan in mind when she saw a round gun barrel pointed right between her eyes.

It was the muzzle of an RPD light machine gun, a mere six feet from her face.

"Well, this is a problem," said the beautiful owner of the gun. Contrary to what her comment suggested, she looked utterly cool and in control. There wasn't the tiniest hint of fury over the slaughter of one of her precious teammates.

She was very, very calm.

Her eyes were not crinkled with a smile. There was only the faintest hint of amusement on her lips.

Ooh, how lovely. This is what they call an "archaic smile," right? It looks even better on a beautiful woman.

Which is what makes it so terrifying!! Llenn shrieked internally but did not say aloud.

Instead, she said the line she'd been prepared to say: "'If our teammates located elsewhere are shooting one another without knowing about us, there's no blaming each other'…right?"

They were Vivi's own words from not that long ago. A perfect quotation, word for word, in fact. The kind of thing you wouldn't think you'd need to memorize.

But Llenn thought, *If I don't say this now, I might be dead.*

"...All right. No blaming each other. Besides, I don't exactly want all of us to wind up dead here," Vivi said, raising her gun.

"Hmm?" Llenn replied. Something caught her attention.

"Agreed," said Boss, slowly lifting herself from Llenn's lap and revealing the object that was tucked into her left hand. Then it all made sense.

At some point, Boss had pulled out the grand grenade. If Vivi had decided to fire her machine gun to get rid of Llenn and her likely future opponent of Boss, all three of them would have died together.

Once again, Boss had saved her life.

Thank you, thank you, thank you! Llenn screamed internally. Another part of her mind, however, was focused on something that didn't really matter at the moment.

If that had happened, who would have gotten the last attack on me and earned the one million ye—I mean, hundred million credits? Would it have been Vivi? Or Boss?

And also, if I off myself in SJ5, do I get the hundred million credits? Not that I would...

She managed to shove all these thoughts out of her mind and give back to Vivi what she'd been meaning to return. She grabbed the LED light on the hood of her poncho and tossed it underhand to Vivi.

She caught it and put it into her chest rig. "The next time we meet, we'll be enemies."

"Got it."

Vivi motioned with the end of her shortened RPD. As Llenn got to her feet, she reached out with the silenced barrel of her P90 and tapped it against the other woman's gun.

Clink.

The metal made a nice, ringing sound.

Once Vivi's figure had vanished into the mist for good, Llenn sucked in a huge breath.

Hfffffffffff.

And then let it out.

"Fukaaaaaaaaaaaaaaaaaaaaaaa!"

"Eep!" Boss, who was taken by surprise at close range, winced.

It was a choice of action that could easily be overheard by enemies, but that was far from Llenn's chief concern at this moment. If she didn't do it, they could be bombarded at any moment by a fresh rain of reloaded grenades—twelve of them.

Fukaziroh's explosions had reduced the house to its foundation and momentarily blown the mist clear, but the haze had since rushed back to fill the space.

Llenn's range of vision was maybe a hundred feet at best. She had no idea where Fukaziroh was, of course. She was presumably on the other side of the foundation and not that far away.

So the only option was to shout.

"Ohhhhhhhhhhhhhhhhhhhhhhhhhhhhhh?" came Fukaziroh's skeptical voice out of the gloom, like a foghorn. "Is that you-uuuuuu, Lleeeeeeeeeeeeeeeeeeeeeeeenn?"

"Yeaaaaaaaaaaaaaaaaaaaaaaaaaaaaaaaaaaaaaaaaaaaaaaaaah!"

"You're not a ghoooooooooooooooooooooooooooooooooost?"

"I almost was because of youuuuuuuuuuuuuuuuuuuuuuuuuu!"

"Oh maaaan! I could have been riiiiiiiiiiiiiiiiiiiiiiiiiiiiiiiiiiiich!"

"Screw youuuuuuuuuuuuuuuuuuuuuuuuuuuuuuuuuuuuuuuuuuuuu!"

Llenn rushed toward the voice, holding her P90 at the ready. Boss followed behind her.

"I'll go right."

"I'll take the left, then," Boss said.

Thanks to all the stupid noise they were making, any nearby enemies would surely be aware that Llenn was in the area. Their eyes were going to be replaced by yen symbols.

Keeping an eye on the sides between the two of them, prepared for the possibility that someone could burst out of the mist at any moment, Llenn and Boss crossed the home they had briefly occupied, which was now just a flat foundation.

"If I can use it, I'm taking that," Boss said.

On the right side of their path, Shinohara lay dead with a tag rotating over his head. At his side was a 7.62 mm machine gun, the M60E3.

The reloading system on his back had been destroyed by the grenade hit, but he seemed to still have plenty of ammunition belts. The gun was intact, too.

If they picked it up, it would be a very powerful weapon gained for free, but there was no point if you couldn't use it.

"Fukaaaaaaaaaaaaaaaaaaaaaaa! I'm heading your way, so don't shoot!"

"I guess we'll have to seeeeeeeeee about thaaaaaaaaaaaaaaa-aaaaaaaaat!"

Llenn ran toward the voice, which seemed to be to the east through the fog. Around the area were several leveled homes due to the shock wave of the self-detonation perpetrated by that member of Team DOOM. It left them as nothing but foundations and rubble.

There was no cover to hide behind or use to shield oneself from shots. It might as well have been a flat field.

They had traveled maybe a hundred feet through the mist.

"Hey, Llenn! I see her! This way! Hurry up!"

Llenn followed the voice and found her at last. The figure up ahead could only be Fukaziroh.

In the foundation of one of the houses blown away by the blast, there was a little basement. It had a cramped, steep set of stairs that could barely fit one person, leading down to a little underground space about the size of a single tatami mat.

It was so tiny, it made you wonder what the design intended for people to do in such a space. The developers were likely just too lazy to go to the trouble of designing an entire basement, data-wise.

In the midst of that space huddled tiny Fukaziroh. She popped her head out of the rectangular opening, which was exposed to the outside without any house around it anymore.

There was a smirk on her lips.

"Yo, Llenn! And, oh…I thought there was a female gorilla hanging around behind you, but it's just Boss. Glad to see you both alive and kicking."

"Same to you," replied Boss with a smile.

Llenn boldly glared at Fukaziroh. "Yes, we're alive! But I thought I was going to die!"

"Yeah, you said that already. Look, I'm sorry. I never would have dreamed that you'd be working with Vivi like that."

"We just ran into each other at random and temporarily teamed up! And thanks to you, that's all been ruined!"

"Listen, I know I've been tellin' you this for over ten years, but…if anyone's with Vivi in a game, the flat truth is that I'm gonna attack them, even if it turns out to be you…"

"You've never said that! And VR games haven't even been around that long!"

"Hey, don't sweat the details! So I assume that Vivi perished in my attack of righteous fury?"

"No, she's alive. Like us, she jumped out of the house and ran before the grenades hit. It was a really close call."

"Ah. But then you finished her off after that, right? Cut off her head, maybe?"

"I let her go."

"What the hell were you thinkiiiiiing?!"

"That's what I'm saaaaaaayiiiiing! If you hadn't shot Shinohara, you could have spent all the remaining time until two o'clock in a safe house with a team of crack snipers!"

"I'd rather die than be on a team with herrrr! I teamed up with Shinohara so I could shoot Vivi in the back! I had him all fooled because of the Shinohara connection! Now I've wasted my plasma grenades!"

"No, we'll get them back. Ugh, we can talk about this later!" Llenn snapped, quickly patching her comm to connect to Fukaziroh again. The connection to Vivi and David had been lost when fate broke them apart.

"Can you hear me?!"

"Sure can!"

Now Llenn, Fukaziroh, and Boss were on the same channel.

"There's no time to sit around and relax. The scan's already started," said Boss, tense and alert.

Llenn glanced quickly at her watch. "Ugh!"

It was five seconds past 1:40.

She had totally missed the vibration she'd set for thirty seconds before the scan started. She hadn't had the frame of mind for it. Because of Fukaziroh!

Watching the scanner, Boss announced calmly, "We've got Fuka's map added now. The north side is much more filled in. What is this, train tracks? That aside, there are three leader marks near us... I don't know any of them. I assume there are other enemies around, too, of course."

And then, more bitterly, she said, "They'll all be rushing toward us in moments, I'm sure."

Fukaziroh added gleefully, "Because of Llenn's bounty!"

It's your fault! Llenn kept herself from snapping. Half of it was Llenn's fault. That much was certain.

"There are going to be enemies in any direction we run, and they'll come from all directions, too. Of course, none of them are likely to be our friends, so we can just kill everyone we see without a second thought..."

Boss was right. None of the idiots who were going to charge Llenn in this situation were members of LPFM or SHINC. Her teammates knew it would lead to a battle, and they'd get mistaken for an enemy and shot at.

Although perhaps some of her teammates *would* shoot the people going after Llenn, from behind. Pitohui. Shirley. Oh man, they would *so* do that.

"That aside," Boss asked, "What do we do?"

It was a very disadvantageous situation.

They had only three people.

And one of them had an extremely enticing bounty on her head.

They were surrounded by enemies. Attempting to flee in any direction would mean certain conflict.

While the fog was thick, the terrain was flat, with almost nothing to hide behind. They could try to squeeze into the tiny basement space, but the moment they were found, they'd be helpless.

Llenn alone might have been able to pick a direction and rush past any enclosing circle. But it would be much, much less likely for all three of them to get through unharmed.

Llenn needed to make a decision.

Llenn made a decision.

It took zero point two seconds. They had no time to waste.

She waved her left hand to remove the poncho she'd been wearing this whole time, then shouted, "Fuka! We managed to meet up again… It's time to do the switchy thing with the alternate gear! It'll work in this terrain!"

"Ha-haaa! I thought you'd say that, pardner. Now's the time for our new killer technique. Let's show off the benefits of our after-school detention training!"

"What?" asked Boss, alarmed.

Their gear-switch was probably supposed to be the ace up their sleeve. And they were doing it already? What was this "new killer technique"?

She had no idea what it could be. But it was *surely* going to turn out to be the one means Llenn had found that would help them survive this desperate situation.

Llenn looked up into Boss's eyes and said, "I want you to stay hidden in this basement for a while! If you're too near…the consequences could be extremely dangerous! We're going to go buck wild out there, so I don't think they'll find you down here!"

"All right… I want to ask what it is you're going to do…"

"No time!"

"Didn't think so."

"If we survive as planned, I'll tell you what it is!"

"Looking forward to it. Good luck."

Boss swiftly turned on her heel and took Fukaziroh's place in the basement shelter. The stairs were there, so once she was underneath, they could put some boards over the space to hide it.

If anyone tried to get in, she could shoot them with the Vintorez, so she'd be safe for a while. A grenade tossed down there might be trouble, but she could worry about that if it happened.

"I'm sure the enemies will be coming after us, but if anything happens, tell us," said Llenn, now dressed in her most characteristic pink battle fatigues.

Anything could mean a super-dangerous foe or a friend in disguise—literally anything. Boss got the gist of it.

"All right. But I'll stay quiet because I don't want to mess you up."

"Thanks!"

Their comms were still linked, so Llenn and Boss finished their conversation, and Boss retreated fully under the basement opening. A gorilla silently vanished from the misty lot.

The teeny-tiny combo of Llenn and Fukaziroh were left alone in the haze, surrounded by a devastated suburban street.

Below her helmet, Fukaziroh's mouth curled into a leering smile.

"Hey, pardner… Do you remember the catchphrase we agonized over all night…when we brainstormed it together?"

Below her pink cap, Llenn's mouth smirked as she chuckled.

"I sure do remember…that we didn't come up with anything!"

Llenn and Fukaziroh waved their left hands in unison to call up their game windows.

There was now a GEAR-SWITCH button that hadn't been there before, which they hit in perfect sync.

*   *   *

"The time is 1:40! It seems there's some action on the field!"

A man dressed in brown camo was hissing under his breath.

He carried an SDF-issue Type 89 5.56 mm rifle, with the folding stock.

Yes, it was him. Thane, the live commentator.

In the midst of wrecked houses and milky-white fog, he stood, surrounded by several other players.

Five yards to the right of Thane was a man in green camo with an AK-74, and beyond him was a man in reddish-brown camo, faded by the fog. About ten yards behind them was a man in the US Marines camo pattern holding an M40A3 sniper rifle.

About five yards to the left of Thane was another player holding a Croatian VHS-2 assault rifle.

Yes, he too had joined forces with players from other teams, and they were fanned out in a formation that gave them just enough visibility of one another that they could proceed slowly but securely.

"The pink shrimp might be around. We're going right for the spot we saw the LPFM dot!"

They were on their way toward Llenn's position.

A bit earlier, during the forty minutes between the beginning of the game and the present moment, Thane executed his own particular survivalist methods upon starting in a forest of huge, vine-laden trees growing in black dirt.

Meaning that just after learning of the special rules and losing contact with his team at 1:10, he loudly called out with his name and location, flickering the flashlight he'd brought and generally drawing as much attention as he possibly could in a bizarre mix of Japanese and English vocabulary.

"*Hey! Everybody!* Listen, *please*! I beg of you, *listen*! I'm talking to the alliance of gamers who say *fuck you* to these shitty rules! Would you like to join me? *Say yes!* I'm Thane! Thane, the commentator! Anybody want to be in one of my videos? Got any lonely *rabbits* out there running away and trying not to die? C'mon, join me!"

In a sense it was a gamble—a desperate play that could have gotten him immediately shot and killed…but this time, it just so happened to work.

Someone saw the white light, recognized that it was not a muzzle flash, and decided to call out from a distance, "Oh, it's you! Fine, I guess I'll team up with you. C'mon, let's do this."

"*Welcome,* sir!"

A team of one became two.

And then…

"I'll do it! These rules suck, man! Let me join up!"

"Yahoo! Anyone else out there? Anyone wanna be our *friend*?!"

"Me, me! Don't shoot me, okay?"

"Welcome, welcome, one and all!"

He repeated his pitch over and over, and by 1:23, he had succeeded in gathering a battalion of nineteen men, including himself. Along the way, no one took advantage of their increased visibility to attack. Thane's wild idea had been a wild success.

The teams represented in this forest gathering were impressively varied.

Not a single pair of players was from the same original team. Considering that each group of six was scattered as widely as possible across the map, that was to be expected.

In terms of recognizable players, the one in the reddish-brown camo with the AC-556F rifle was from the team that tried to reach out and form a patchwork alliance in SJ2. He'd been in the game since SJ1. That was a team that had a long and boring Squad Jam history.

There was also a member of the Ray Gun Boys (RGB), who insisted on using optical guns despite the disadvantages. They had been given a good chance to show off in SJ4, though, and they had made it a memorable one.

According to him, the teams that Fire had recruited for SJ4 hadn't shown up in this game at all.

Of course, Thane and the others had no idea those teams had merely been mercenaries whom Fire Nishiyamada hired for the sake of personal romance. Whatever those players thought of their job once they learned the actual result of it was unknown. Maybe they did their best to console him?

The man with the G3A3ZF automatic sniper rifle and the West German army uniform was one of the members of NSS, the historical cosplay group. There was also a member of T-S, the sci-fi-suited team and one-time champions. He stood out, both in style and in height.

There was a player dressed in a light outdoorsy style, as though he were about to take a nice day hike. His gun was an M2 Carbine, a pretty old-fashioned light rifle used by the Americans during World War II.

The others were either impressed or annoyed that he had survived the preliminary round, but they understood when he explained that his teammates were all heavy firepower types and he just took it easy. His *GGO* playstyle was to keep it light and nimble. He was just enjoying a little walk.

In addition, there were other folks who had never spoken to one another but *had* been in plenty of death matches.

"Oh yeah, that was me who killed you that one time."

"It was a nice kill. Good job."

They sounded like old classmates at a reunion. The men in the mist were having a grand old time, despite uniformly being enemies. It was one of the strange bits of camaraderie that Squad Jam fostered. It'd probably be fun to do an IRL meetup.

Of course, none of the nineteen were from LPFM, SHINC, MMTM, or ZEMAL. And they wouldn't be.

"There's no way those guys will pop up. I'm guessin' they're all keeping their heads down somewhere," said someone, to firm and unanimous agreement.

"The first target for us should be LPFM, who are just to the west of us," said the man in reddish-brown camo, who seemed to enjoy calling the shots.

"But the pink demon isn't in this Squad Jam, bro. Her mysterious absence is a major blow, whether it's out of fear or something else. This is a hard, cold place of strife, and that's the brutal truth of life," Thane replied.

One man ignored him and said, "About that... I think it's a trap that M and Pitohui set up. Either she was already there ahead of time or jumped into the pub at exactly 12:50 so no one saw her."

"Ahhhhhh. But the question is, why? Second to last letter of the alphabet, *Y*."

"Because it's a plot to confuse us and make us think the pink demon isn't here. They'd do something like that, wouldn't they?"

Yes, they would. They absolutely would.

All in attendance agreed on that point.

And yet...

Oh, they figured it out.

Not a single one of them could have guessed that Pitohui herself was in the woods nearby, eavesdropping on their conversation. She had them roughly in her sights at present.

Pitohui had started in this forest and chosen to stay hidden for a while. But when she learned there was a group making lots of noise to pull more players in, she couldn't sit still anymore and decided to follow their trail.

She was dressed in a camo poncho, lying flat on the damp earth and listening intently to their chat. If she wanted to, she could use the KTR-09 rifle in her hands to fire until its seventy-five-round drum magazine was empty and take out at least half of them. But she didn't.

She held it in.

They were going to make things fun for Llenn, after all.

"All right, so we're in agreement on heading west to vanquish LPFM! Yes? Agreed? No objections, gentlemen?" Thane asked. There was no rebuttal. "Good! Then let's go get that hundred million! Rejoice, regroup, and rejoin our fates! We set our sights on the pink devil! We fight back the punk devils! We spit fire with our assault rifles! And we'll overcome all the trifles!"

His overexcited rap concluded at 1:27:34.

Which was the exact same moment that Team DOOM set off its major blast.

Despite the explosion occurring very far away, the light reached them in the forest, and over ten seconds later, the blast wind as well. What had been an utterly still world was instantly punched through by air pressure, shaking and rocking the trees.

Several players were truly shocked by the blast, which was unlike anything they'd experienced before in *GGO*. They thought their AmuSpheres were going to shut down and kick them out of Squad Jam. Thankfully, that did not happen.

When the forest was calm and the blue sky was once again full of fog, Thane jabbered, "Everyone all right? What a blast! An explosion of shock! It must have been *them*—the suicide bombers! If I die, I'm going to come back as a ghost to haunt you!"

"So they're here, too," said someone else. "If they exploded there, it means none of the other five are close! And even if there's another enemy nearby, they can't possibly kill all of us at once! That's good news for us!"

He and Thane and the other seventeen headed for the residential neighborhood.

Have a good trip! Beat Llenn while you're there! Pitohui thought. She stayed in the forest.

And then it was 1:40.

"The pink shrimp might be there. Let's make for the signal from LPFM on the map!"

During the fourth scan, the allied team learned that LPFM was close by, and they executed their devious plan.

"It's Operation Surround Her as a Group!"

As they left the woods, they fanned out as wide as they could in a plot to keep Llenn contained. More specifically, they spread out just far enough to where they could still see another member on the right and left, front and rear, and they slowly but carefully closed in.

They gave themselves numbers from one to nineteen, starting from the north end of the fan. It was easier to call out numbers than one another's names when they were all connected over comms. They weren't going to memorize that many names in such a short time anyway.

One through six were on the right side of the advancing group, seven through thirteen were in the middle, and fourteen through nineteen were the left wing.

If someone got shot, he would either call out his number before he died or one of his teammates would do it. In the mist, you had to be able to see a foe to shoot them, so if one of their number went down, it would mean an enemy was nearby, guaranteed, and then the players on the sides or rear would open fire in return.

The idea was that blanket fire in a space where you couldn't see was guaranteed to do damage to the enemy. It was the most secure and effective plan for a group that was certain to have a numerical advantage.

The players with the best shooting ability were placed on the right and left edges of the formation. They were folks with machine guns or high-output assault rifles.

Thane kept his voice down as they walked. "The tension in the mist here is absolutely palpable. Nineteen brave heroes are making their way forward to vanquish a pink demon who may or may not be there. It's very much like the domed jungle in SJ2, only this time we have our comms hooked up! They were unable to achieve secure communication back then, which led to a very tragic outcome. Speaking of which, when did it become possible to tune your comms with the enemy? I suppose that's not important right now."

Thane was tenth of the group. He had his Type 89 rifle's safety-slash-selector switch set to "auto" and held at his waist, so he was prepared to fire at a moment's notice.

"So will the pink demon worth a hundred million credits show her face...? If so, when...where...and how many?"

"Wait...there's more than one Llenn?"

"Does that mean double the bounty?"

"I wish there were ten of her, then."

Everyone else could hear his commentary through the comm, of course, so his new companions had plenty of replies for him.

"Thanks for the comments, folks. Remember to hit LIKE and SUBSCRIBE."

"C'mon, don't make us laugh. We gotta stay quiet."

"Jawohl!"

"Why are you speaking German?"

"Because I don't know how to say, 'Yes, sir,' in Russian!"

"Makes sense."

Thane's group continued their advance.

Slowly and quietly.

They'd already moved past the forest where they started, into the emptied parts of the neighborhood that the blast had flattened. There wasn't much to see, aside from cracked asphalt, plain dirt, and flat home foundations.

Some of the group had started here, so they had their own map data and eyewitness memory to go by. They said there had been multiple houses here earlier.

And a single blast did this much damage? How much explosive powder did they bring in here? DOOM is crazy.

"Should be right around here..." Thane heard someone murmur. This was the place where the LPFM dot had been just one minute ago, at 1:40.

"Everyone, stop for a moment. Do you see anything? Hear anything? They might be hiding under rubble, totally still. If you see anything strange, speak up quietly," said the man in reddish-brown camo, followed by several seconds of silence.

Thane peered for all he was worth. He kept his ears finely tuned.

But nothing was amiss.

The environment was littered with foundations, blasted lumber, window frames, shards of brick, scrap metal that had once belonged to a car, and something that looked like a metal box.

"Hmm? What do you suppose that is?" Thane said. Then he realized that no one else could see it, and explained, "About ten yards in front of me, there's a box with four dull gray metal sides, about five feet tall, with something like a lid placed on top of it... Is that some part of a house?"

It looked just like some kind of industrial product.

The shape was like a tower or the tip of a chimney, only made out of strangely clean metal, with a bit of a taper at the top.

The player just to his left was able to see it, too. "Oh, that's an American-style large trash can. It's just been knocked over so that it's upside-down. Hard to tell at first."

"Ah, I see. Yes, it does look like a trash can now. And it doesn't seem to be moving," Thane reported.

The man in reddish-brown camo said, "Then we'll move forward slowly. If anything moves, open fire and tell the group. We're getting our ammo back anyway. Let's use it up."

Got it, they thought. Nineteen players resumed their forward progress.

They were as slow and methodical as if they were mowing the lawn. They would move forward, stop, listen for sounds, take a look, then move again. The view within the mist did not change much.

It was extremely nerve-racking, knowing that bullets or pink demons might come rushing through the milky curtain at any moment.

But their numerical superiority and the allure of a hundred million credits gave them courage and kept them going.

If Llenn was here, she might possibly be working with another teammate, but the chances of her teaming up with multiple other groups like he was doing was low, Thane decided. Most other people would rather have the hundred million credits anyway.

Thane proceeded another ten yards, then observed his surroundings again.

The object he'd taken for a trash can earlier was now at close range, and he could see the stenciled paint on the side. It read COMBUSTIBLES but was flipped upside down and nearly faded out.

It was a long English vocabulary word that most Japanese people did not know, but the meaning was simple: trash you could burn.

So it is a stupid trash can in the end! Got me worried for nothing, my metal friend! Thane rhymed in his head. He was just walking past the trash can when he died.

"Huh? No way! Why?! How?!"

It was only when he appeared in the black space before the start of the game, the waiting area, that Thane understood that he had died and been bounced out of SJ5.

"Hang on a second! Seriously, why? *Por qué? Pourquoi?*"

He just didn't understand.

Thane had absolutely no idea how he had been determined dead.

Normally if you got shot in *GGO*, your body registered an impact vibration, even if it was an insta-kill shot, which didn't leave you with the opportunity to twitch a finger.

If you got shot in the middle of the forehead with a rifle round, you'd feel a virtual sensation like someone flicking you hard with a finger. The pain was very temporary, and it wouldn't vibrate your brain, but you would notice it.

The same was true of getting stabbed or blown up. All physical sensations were re-created virtually and sent to the brain.

But in this case, Thane felt absolutely nothing. There was no bodily sensation.

Though he wouldn't exactly consider it bragging, Thane was something of an expert on dying in *GGO*. He would know what it felt like to be OHKO'd, because it had happened to him so many times.

Yet this time, Thane didn't even have the chance to feel any virtual pain. He died as abruptly as if he were a TV channel that had just been changed, and he'd been whisked off the SJ5 map just as quickly.

How could he have died to cause this phenomenon?

"I'm dead, y'all! I got sent back to the waiting room! But how did I die? Why did I die? What in the world is this strange sensation…? Is it…love? No, no, it's not. Love is much more floaty, like a throbbing in your chest…"

His recording was still ongoing, so Thane didn't miss a beat in continuing the running commentary.

Then he came to a realization: It would be easy to find out how he died. Thane waved his arm to call up his player window, pressed buttons here and there, and then projected the official commentated SJ5 video onto the wall of the waiting area.

Two large screens filled the space.

On the left was the live stream of the event as it was unfolding. On the right was a replay of his death. In the bottom right corner of each video was a label that said either LIVE or REPLAY.

Almost immediately, Thane saw, by complete coincidence, the events on each screen matched each other. In other words, what was happening live was perfectly in sync with the replay.

"Ohhh…"

From the seam of the "trash can," a pale beam of light thrust outward about three feet—the sci-fi lightsaber of *GGO*, the sharp edge of a photon sword…

On the left screen was one of his companions, and on the right screen was himself. Both players walked right into the path of the blade and got their heads cut off.

The metal plate on the bottom of the upturned trash can pushed upward, revealing a pink object with the plate on its head that popped up and swung a photon sword with tremendous speed.

The beheading went from the back of the head through the eyes.

That would immediately cause the brain to stop functioning, leaving it with no time to even simulate any virtual pain.

And it explained the instantaneous warp-like death. It made sense. It made way too much sense.

A beat or two after he saw the video, Thane said, "Oh! Eureka!"

The pink shape, of course, was the pink demon: Llenn.

"Everybody, run! She's inside that trash can! Er, it's not a trash can—it's just a thing! She's hiding there! Look out! Dangerrrr!" he screamed.

But of course, no one still in the game could hear him.

"That's three!" Fukaziroh shouted.

"Yesss!" Llenn added, riding on her shoulders.

Llenn and Fukaziroh were inside the object that Thane and his companions believed was a trash can.

It was four metal plates with a fifth one as a lid, and with both of them inside, they were packed about as tight as could be. Of course, it was not a trash can. If they were to give it a name…

"Let's go, *Pretty Miyu!*"

"Is that the name? It's too long! Let's just call it the *PM!*"

"Ew, like the afternoon?!"

It was the *PM.*

The inner workings of the *PM* were actually quite simple. You could easily make it yourself with a bit of money, so it would be worth trying the next time you're in *GGO.*

First get some sturdy but lightweight pipes. In the real world, carbon would be best, but *GGO* has some mysterious materials that are even lighter and tougher, so use those instead.

Then carefully and skillfully bend the pipes and combine them to create the frame of a large trash can structure. Of course, since it's such a hard material, the existence of fashioning commands in the virtual world makes it so much easier to cut and bend things, as well as connect them again.

There you go, a trash can frame. Now you're almost done.

However, in this state, it's just a large cage. We'll need to put on the finishing touches.

This is when you firmly attach bulletproof plates on each of the four sides of the frame. You'll need to carefully size them so that the edges are perfectly tight with no gaps in between. In those seams, you'll apply an adhesive used for spaceships (according to the game) and metal fixtures to attach the plates to the pipe frame.

Then you'll want to fashion another plate to be the bottom of the trash can. But this one, you don't stick on. Although it's the bottom, you're going to flip the structure over, so technically it's a lid.

Thanks to the pipe frame running to the corners, this lid can be lifted evenly and silently, without slipping off to the side. The frame also needs four tires, little rubber ones like the kind on grocery carts, for one very specific purpose.

"Here we gooooo!"

By pushing for all she was worth, Fukaziroh could essentially move the *PM* at the same speed that she could run. It was something that only Fukaziroh could do because she was such a musclehea— er, because she was so physically disciplined.

The tires, too, had a special mechanism. Two pipes inside the structure ran from front to back right at Fukaziroh's shoulder height, so when she stood up, her shoulders would lift them just a bit.

Thanks to the bends in the pipes and the lever mechanism, it would lower the *PM*'s tires slightly, until they made contact with the ground. When she crouched a bit, the tires would lift again and put the outer plates in contact with the ground. At that point, it would look like nothing else but a trash can placed upside down.

Since there was no gap between the bottom and the ground, no bullets could ricochet and get inside the box.

Llenn's feet were resting on that part of the inner frame. She was just riding on it. Fukaziroh was piloting the can, while Llenn was crouching over her shoulders, like getting a piggyback ride.

*   *   *

"Fuka! Fifteen degrees left, five yards! No obstacles! Full speed!"

"Roger!"

Llenn was peering out through a tiny gap left under the lid so she could give instructions to Fukaziroh, who was running blind in the middle of the darkened can.

On the inside where she could see, there were numbers indicating angles, so she just pointed in a direction and then ran.

I'll have your life!

When right next to a foe, Llenn would flip up the lid and use her photon sword, the Muramasa F9, to slice them through the torso or neck.

There went another man, sacrificed to honor the God of *Gun Gale*.

This was a combination strategy devised, planned, bought, and even constructed by M: their second gear loadout.

The photon sword that had been borrowed from Pitohui and the relatively light vehicle pipes were Llenn's second gear set, carried by Fukaziroh.

Thanks to her higher carrying capacity, Fukaziroh's second set was the heavier metal plates, carried by Llenn.

When they performed the gear-switch function, the items materialized, which they then combined and used together. Something that only they could do, a combined ultra technique forged of pure friendship.

The Pseudo-Trash-Can Two-Man Human-Powered Armored Vehicle.

Otherwise known as the *PM*.

At the point that they'd slaughtered the fourth person, the men in the area finally began to realize that the simple "trash can" was, in fact, their enemy.

"There's someone in there! It went toward the right wing!" said the man in reddish-brown camo, watching the trash can move from his left side toward his right. He opened fire with his AC-556F.

There were still allies through the mist and elsewhere nearby, but there was no time to be cautious now. If someone got hit by a stray bullet, well—my bad, bro.

The bullets he shot at the trash can all spattered against its surface—*cla-cla-cla-cla-clang!*—and ricocheted off.

"Wha—?!"

He fired and fired some more, to which the trash can turned on its heel—well, since it didn't have any visible feet, let's just say it rotated 180 degrees—and began to slide over the ground toward him.

Shooting had only revealed his location to the target.

The can was unbothered by slight imperfections in the ground surface and easily made its way over rubble, approaching in silence. It was extremely unsettling.

"Wha—?!"

He kept shooting. He shot and shot, but all the bullets were easily repelled. Soon his thirty-shot magazine was empty, and the can was still coming.

"Aaaah!"

He rushed to replace the magazine, and his handiwork was fairly dexterous, but the trash can was already right upon him.

The lid popped up several centimeters. From inside the can, he heard an adorable voice call out, "Yaaah." And then a pale blade of light emerged and ran him straight through from stomach to back.

"What the hell is that? That's not fair! I mean, I guess it is fair technically!"

In the waiting area, Thane watched the feed. He continued to watch. He had no choice but to watch as his companions were slain one after the other.

"No, I changed my mind. It's definitely not fair!"

＊　　＊　　＊

One of the players in the allied team fired his Remington Model 870 shotgun as fast and often as he could.

The Remington Model 870 was renowned as a hunting shotgun, but his gun was outfitted with tactical items like an extended magazine tube, an accessory rail, and dot sights—making it a combat model.

It was a pump-action gun, meaning that after firing it, he would pull back on the pump to expel the empty cartridge, then push it forward again to load the next shot. Every use of the gun involved a lot of movement with that left hand.

He was firing slugs—single bullets sized for shotguns—that were big and heavy and as powerful as rifle rounds at close range. Each one hit the target, and each one bounced harmlessly off of it.

The trash can took each shot without wobbling and continued to slide forward over the ground, from left to right, about ten yards away from him.

Then, at that very moment, a glowing blade appeared from a crack between the lid and the body. And one of the companions he'd just met today, who was trying to flee the area, got sliced into two pieces, his upper and lower halves crumpling to the ground.

"What the hell...?"

Shock overrode any kind of momentary mourning. Then the trash can brandishing a blade came rushing toward *him*.

"Aaah! Stay away!"

It was too sudden to call out the number of his dead teammate, and though he tried to pack more shells into his Remington's empty tube, it was already too late.

The trash can knew he couldn't fire the gun he was carrying, so its lid slowly, silently rose upward, until his eyes met those of the person inside.

Within the darkness, he glimpsed a pink hat and a pair of gleaming eyes watching him closely.

He stopped reloading, knowing it was pointless, and mumbled, "P-pink demon…"

"I wish you wouldn't call me that," said a cute voice, followed by a photon sword that viciously stabbed him through the throat.

She really is a demon! he would have shouted if his vocal cords had still been intact.

"Right wing, what happened?!"

Slightly earlier, the nineteenth man—meaning the one on the farthest left point of their formation—yelled into his comm for clarification and received no answer.

He'd been hearing confused shouts and death screams for quite a while now, and to his right through the mist, in the direction they were traveling, there were raucous, wild gunshots.

"What is happening…?"

It was impossible to tell from where he was hearing the noises.

He would have liked if they'd at least explained how they were being killed, what kind of enemy it was, or what weapon they were using, before they all died.

But maybe the situation did not give them the wherewithal to explain.

In other words, it was bad.

Number Eighteen said, "Whatever! There's clearly an enemy nearby! Probably that pink demon worth a hundred million! Let's go! Everyone, move slightly closer together!"

"Okay!"

The six men from Fourteen to Nineteen started converging. They each turned ninety degrees to the right and arranged themselves in a tight—though still a bit loose—formation, then resumed activity.

"I'll take lead, then!" said the T-S member, who was Seventeen.

"Great! Thanks!"

He was confident in his defense, so he would surely soak up some of the damage for the others.

Every other man in the group thought, *Wow, he's great to have on our side... My team really needs someone with that armor equipped, too...*

Likewise, the T-S man had a feeling that all of them were thinking that. *But scraping together a whole set of this armor is gonna cost you a whoooole lotta money. You got the guts for that, boys?*

So the sci-fi soldier took the lead, rare HK GR9 5.56 mm machine gun at the ready, and the others lined up behind him. Each one maintained a distance of ten feet from the player in front of him.

Although they hadn't decided on it, if the man in front was pointing his gun toward the right, the man behind would focus on the left instead. These were the instincts of veteran *GGO* players.

They would have liked to run right to the location in question, but that would involve too much risk, so caution demanded they take it slowly. You didn't know what might come rushing out of the fog anyway.

The pack traveled at no faster than a speedwalk, following nothing but the occasional gunfire of their companions for clues.

Then a voice through the comm said, "Enemy alert! There's some kind of weird blocky thing—"

And it stopped there.

Oh, he's dead now. RIP. Still got a chance for that hundred million credits, though.

Five seconds later, someone else said, "What's this? That's not the pink demon..."

There was more gunfire and then: "Hey! There's a boxy-looking—*aagh!*"

The sound stopped there.

No, seriously, what is happening out there...?

To the six unfortunate men who had no idea how to answer that question, the events happening in the mist represented pure terror.

They'd heard Thane's conversation about the trash can earlier, but none of them were able to put two and two together that it was an enemy trap. Instead, their imaginations ran wild, filling their heads with visions of some massive monster preying on helpless humans just out of sight.

They soon found themselves looking higher up in the air. The toes of their boots caught on rubble, threatening to unbalance them.

"P-pink demon…," a voice repeated. Whomever it was did not speak again.

There was no denying that the demon worth a hundred million credits was among them.

And the group with the T-S member at the lead decided…

"New group! Stop for a sec!"

"You got it."

Llenn spotted the shape of a sci-fi soldier through the mist and gave a quick command to her driver, Fukaziroh, with whom she was currently in more or less intimate contact.

"It's a T-S guy."

They were larger than other players and had an identifiable silhouette, so it was easy to recognize them.

Fukaziroh stopped walking and lowered her shoulders so that the tires were hidden and the trash can was stabilized. Llenn lowered her head until the lid was closed. It was shut tight, without even a millimeter of a gap. Now it was nothing but a suspicious-looking trash can turned upside down in the street.

Hunching down, Llenn had her eyes at the perfect level to see out if she opened the lid the tiniest crack. It was a gap that extended to all four sides, which made it convenient for looking in all directions, but it was also the *PM*'s one vulnerable point.

There was a greater than zero chance that, by sheer coincidence, a bullet smaller than the crack could enter through it. But if it happened, you just had to tip your cap. That's some lucky shootin'.

Llenn observed the group through the fog.

"Twenty yards. Coming almost directly for us. T-S machine gunner in the lead. Vertical line starting three yards behind him. I can see three, but I bet there's more," she reported, for Fukaziroh's sake.

"Sounds like a lot," her partner replied. "Should we slip past them?"

Llenn considered this and came to an immediate answer. "If they've heard about what we're hiding in…that's bad. The one thing we can't survive is a plasma grenade."

As a matter of fact, the news had *not* been passed on; however, Llenn had no choice but to be cautious.

With how tough the *PM* was, a normal grenade would only knock it over with the force of the explosion. That would be very bad for the two hiding inside, but they wouldn't die instantly.

They had proven this in a joint training exercise after the *PM*'s completion. They called it a bulletproofing test, which mostly consisted of Pitohui chucking a bunch of grenades at them. They got hurtled several yards away. There was a whole lot of head-bonking inside the trash can when that happened. It really hurt.

But a plasma grenade was a different story entirely.

The walls of the *PM* were made of the same spaceship plating as M's shield, the strongest material known in the game. But even that could not withstand the gradual melting effect of the plasma surge.

It wouldn't happen immediately, but depending on the placement of the blast center, a single grenade might be enough to destroy the walls of the vehicle.

"I'm thinking it's not a wise move to do anything right now," Fukaziroh said. The group wouldn't help but notice a trash can sliding around over the ground.

"We're going to do the thing…," Llenn remarked.

"Ah yes, the thing… Which thing?"

"I totally explained it to you! That if we get surrounded, I'll jump out, so you stay in here!"

"Oh, right, you did say that. It was four years ago by now."

"It was *just the other day!*"

Sometimes I can't believe you, Fuka, fumed Llenn as she watched the approaching enemy.

The T-S member was now clearly visible at a distance of about fifteen yards, which meant he could surely see them, too.

If he came closer and showed any signs of recognizing them, Llenn was going to knock the lid off, stand up, and go in for a bloodbath with two photon swords. It was an ultimate technique that used nothing more than Llenn's speed and a pair of lightswords.

"I'm gonna do it…"

"There you go, Battotai. I can remember the Battle of Tabaruzaka like it was yesterday…"

"Where is that?"

"In Kumamoto. From the Satsuma Rebellion."

"Fuka, why are you so weirdly knowledgeable about history at random moments?"

"No idea."

"Well, if I die doing this, you have to survive for me…"

"Come on, pardner. Don't talk like that… You can't die here. How am I going to collect your hundred million?"

"I knew you'd say that."

"What is that?" asked the T-S member at the head of the line.

Through the mist, he could just barely make out a trash can. It was about ten yards away.

"Everyone, stop."

He stayed standing, keeping the machine gun held at his waist, with the muzzle pointed right at the trash can.

It looked like a trash can to him. Although it was faded, COMBUSTIBLES was written on the side. It had probably flipped upside down from the big explosion, which wouldn't be a surprise.

But something was off.

His instincts were telling him that it was just plain *odd*.

"Oh!"

He figured out what it was.

There were visible signs of being hit by gunfire. On a trash can. And the gunshots didn't cause holes. When you fired at a thick metal surface, the bullets would shatter and leave a black stain mark. This trash can had many of those.

So he said, "There's a weird trash can here. I'm gonna try shooting it. If there's any reaction to it, I want you to shoot back."

The men behind him chimed in.

"Roger that."

"Check."

"Yup."

"Okay."

The T-S man put his finger on the GR9's trigger.

And the next moment—*twang!*

Sparks flew from the left temple of his helmet. He'd been hit.

"Rgh!"

But it wasn't enough to kill him.

His rounded helmet was naturally sloped, meaning it had excellent bullet-deflection capabilities, and it ensured the rifle bullet bounced off. It also had firm support around his neck, which softened the impact of the hit. The man inside had to deal with only a bit of pain in his neck.

Then over ten bullet lines appeared through the mist from the left up ahead, reaching for him and his companions.

"Left angle! Enemies! Lots of 'em!"

He opened fire with the GR9 at the base direction of the glowing lines.

The trash can would have to wait.

All of a sudden, things were much livelier outside.

"What's goin' on out there?" asked Fukaziroh, who could not see.

"Lucky us!" Llenn replied, watching through the hole. "T-S got shot before he could shoot us!"

*   *   *

Things had been fairly chaotic already up to that point, but this is where it really ramped up.

In addition to the group sneaking up on Llenn, there was another impromptu tag team that had rushed to her location.

They, too, had no members from LPFM or other friendly teams. Of course they didn't. But they did have the teammates of some folks she had already killed. You could tell by the matching camo. But the players themselves did not realize.

And these were all people so tempted by money that they stopped paying attention to the finer details—and were proactive enough to seize their chance when they thought it had come.

Their misfortune was that they didn't try talking before they started shooting at one another.

"Something crazy's going on outside."

"I can hear it, at least."

Within the universe as Llenn could perceive it, people were dying left and right.

The T-S machine gunner who got hit first was blasting and blasting away, but although his armor deflected many bullets that hit him, it could not prevent the large grenade blast from throwing him skyward.

While its defensive power was high, the suit fell victim to an explosion between the legs, and he hurtled six feet into the air, landed on his head, and flopped to the ground with a DEAD tag over him. Most likely the cause of death was a broken neck. Unlucky guy.

"Shit! Get 'em!"

"You bet!"

"Eat this!"

The men behind him rallied for the sake of the man who'd been their companion for only a few minutes, hoping to avenge his death. They responded to the attack with full force. They really needn't have.

The other side assumed, naturally, that there were many more foes in this direction, and they fought back even harder, too. You couldn't tell who was who through the mist, so they used bullet lines and muzzle flashes to see one another.

Right next to the trash can in which Llenn and Fukaziroh hid, a storm of bullets hurtled back and forth, along with a light show of bullet lines.

It was the start of a very flashy fireworks display.

A battle of group against group, desperate and pitched. The gunshots were wild and frequent, filling the world with noise.

Every few moments, a stray shot would hit the *PM* with a sharp *clang*, shaking the frame and deafening the two girls inside.

"You know, I couldn't help but notice, it's insanely loud when this thing gets shot."

"M says his shield is the same way."

"It needs improving."

"But how? Lining it with soundproofing?"

"Guess there's not enough room for that...but we could play classical music in here, maybe. Or Elza Kanzaki."

"Hmm..."

"Do we need her permission?"

"No, I don't think so."

While Fukaziroh and Llenn enjoyed a casual little chat, the virtual slaughter continued outside.

Through her peephole, Llenn saw a man crawling on hands and knees about fifteen yards away. He was staying low to reduce his target size and creeping closer to the enemy on the left side of her field of view.

In his hand was a convergence grenade, the kind he'd used to blow up T-S a moment earlier. It was a grenade that took only the explosive part from the old-school stick grenades called "potato mashers" and tied them together.

It had excellent explosive power, enough to blow up vehicles. Even the *PM* would be in danger if it had to deal with that.

Please, just don't throw it this way! Llenn prayed. Her plea must have gotten through, because the man suddenly stood up and hurled it for all he was worth, away into the mist.

A beat later, there was an explosion.

"Gyahk!"

There was a scream along with it, and red damage effects spread through the mist. Whomever it was had just gone to Heaven.

"Yessss!"

The man who'd pulled off that incredible blind grenade kill pumped his arm in triumph, just before a bullet went through his head.

"Dammit! They're just normal players like us."

"Where the hell is that pink shrimp?!"

Two men hissed at each other, hiding behind cover.

I'm right here, Llenn thought but could not say.

Because the men were using her very own trash can—pardon, the *PM*—as their shield.

It was a trash can of just the right size, and for some reason, it was blocking bullets for them, so they threw themselves flat on the ground right next to it. And now they were exchanging fire through the mist with their assault rifles.

The one on the right firing an M4A1 was wearing a navy blue camo pattern that made him look like a police tactical unit member. On the left was a man in American desert camo holding a Bushmaster ACR.

They were shooting at full auto into the mist, not knowing if they were hitting anything, and after a few moments, more full auto fire would come back their way.

If they hadn't been able to duck behind the *PM*, they would have died a long time ago. The enemy had pinned down their location and was starting a furious automatic counterattack.

Naturally, being subjected to ten times the gunfire as before, the inside of the *PM* was a deafening clamor. It was like being trapped inside a very small bell that was ringing repeatedly between them.

Ugh, it's so loud!

If she weren't in *GGO*, the sound would have ruptured her eardrums. Llenn cradled her head in her hands, but she couldn't jump out now. She just shrank farther into herself.

She didn't know how many enemies were nearby. Many of them were already dead, that was certain.

Llenn glanced at her watch. After 1:48.

"Shit!"

The man in the desert camo looked ahead as he exchanged the magazine on his ACR, then fired back a few shots at the place where the bullet lines had been.

But the enemy wasn't just sitting in the same spot, of course. His shots were futile.

"Whoa, hold on! Is that you, Hash? I hear that ACR!"

Somewhere through the mist was a real freak. He was able to identify the gun just from the sound it made.

"Oh?" The man he called Hash paused and pulled his finger off the trigger. The world was suddenly quiet. "Hey! That voice! Is that Dane?!" he exclaimed with delight.

"Yeah! I knew it was you, Hash! No way! Hey, don't shoot! Don't shoot! It's just me over here!"

"Got it! There's only two of us, too! Come straight in the direction you were shooting! I'm in front of a weird-looking trash can!"

Having called Dane over, Hash turned to the man with the M4A1 beside him and beamed. "Hey, partner. That's my team-mate. Looks like I'm not dying here quite yet."

"Yeah, it's a relief to hear."

"Only speaking of me and my teammate, though. Sorry, bud."

Brrrat!

Hash pointed his gun at the nearby man and shot him three times. The bullets went right into the other man's heart.

"Damn youuuu! I'll haunt you as a ghooost!" he shouted as he left SJ5 for good.

"Sorry about that. Do your best to move on. May you rest in

peace," said Hash, making a prayer gesture with just one hand. A spinning DEAD tag appeared over the fallen man's head.

"Ah, there you are! Coming, coming!" said a voice, and then another man in the same desert camo came trotting out of the mist. It was a sign they were on the same team, if not partners matching for their date night.

The weapon belonging to the man named Dane was an M249, also known as a Minimi LMG.

The Minimi had way too many models, both in real life and in *GGO*, but Dane's favorite was the vanilla classic.

In other words, the very first Minimi model, the simplest to use and the cheapest to purchase as an item. While its specs were the lowest of any model, many people liked its vibe and its no-frills metal pipe stock.

The newest model wasn't always the ideal when it came to guns. Surprisingly, many people liked choosing older guns on purpose, just because they liked the aesthetics of those items.

He'd been heavily using the gun until moments ago, so the Minimi's barrel was smoking white. If you stuck a piece of meat to it, you could probably put a pretty good grill mark on it.

"What about the others on the team?" asked Dane, who crouched next to the trash can and began to exchange Minimi gun barrels.

Hash kept an eye out on the horizon for him. "You're the only one I've met so far. I teamed up with the commentator guy in the forest, then it turned into a group of nearly twenty, and we were looking to collect Llenn's bounty around here. But instead, everyone went down without realizing why… That wasn't you, was it?"

Dane stuck the fresh barrel on and swung it to the side. "We teamed up in an impromptu group on the highway to the north and then followed the scan…but along the way we heard a gunfight, so we were checking it out from a distance—and just when the action calmed down, we wandered over. I haven't seen the pink shrimp. Awww, dammit. I guess I didn't *need* to fight after all, then."

"Hey, it's all right. We're both alive, and that's worth celebrating. How are your hit points?"

"Took a bit of damage. Still at eighty."

"Sorry about that. Mighta been my shot."

"For this one day, I forgive you," Dane said, beaming, right before his head fell off.

Hash hadn't been watching in the moment, but he *did* notice his friend's head rolling around at his feet.

"Eugh!"

He looked up with a start and saw nothing but a pale blade of light being swung right at him.

"Boss! It's all good now! Come on out!"

At 1:48, near the ten-minute mark, Boss got the all-clear to come out of the cramped basement stairwell.

"Cool." She popped right out.

The first thing she noticed, amid the slightly less dense mist than before, was a bunch of DEAD tags hovering all over the place.

"Talk about fear. Y'all had a massacre up here," she remarked.

"You're a rapper?" Fukaziroh's voice replied.

"Oh, there you are. Ahead on the right, fifteen degrees," Llenn's voice said.

"What the...?"

At this point, Boss noticed a strange garbage can moving in her direction. She very nearly shot at it.

"This is, um, really something..."

Boss was impressed, if somewhat skeptical, of the *PM*.

It did indeed look just like a trash can, but it was probably the only trash can in the entire world with dozens of black marks from deflected bullets on it. In the entire virtual world, that is.

The lid flipped up off the top, and Llenn's head popped out. She

lifted the lid with her hand first, then pushed it loose entirely and tossed it aside.

"Hah!"

Her tiny body jumped and did a flip right out of the trash can. The landing was impeccable. The judges were sure to give her a high score.

"Whew, finally outside again," murmured Fukaziroh, following her out like a woodland creature emerging from hibernation. "Okay, time to put the car back in the garage."

"Good idea."

Fukaziroh and Llenn both waved a hand to call up their game windows.

After they selected the GEAR-SWITCH button, the trash can— better known as the *PM*—vanished, replaced by Llenn's and Fukaziroh's main weapons.

Llenn now had her P90, not the Vorpal Bunnies. Fukaziroh, of course, had her two MGL-140s, the revolving, six-shot grenade launchers.

At that moment, Llenn's wristwatch buzzed, warning her that she had only thirty seconds until the 1:50 scan started.

"Should we watch the fifth scan here?"

"Sure. I don't think there are any enemies around. You killed them all. But maybe we should squeeze into that cellar, just in case," Boss suggested.

"Roger that."

"Okay."

They crammed into the tiny basement.

"Hey, why's it so cramped in here?"

"Because your ass is too big, that's why, Boss."

"Sorry. Good thing you two are so tiny."

"Heh-heh-heh, aw, shucks."

They waited for the fifth scan to arrive.

CHAPTER 7

What Everyone Else Did

SECT.7

CHAPTER 7
What Everyone Else Did

Earlier—much earlier—in time, at the moment of the first scan at 1:10, after losing contact with Llenn, her teammates began their own stories in the mist.

"Let's see."

Pitohui opened her window and flipped through her options until she had the right patterned poncho for her current location: in a forest of massive trees with vines wrapped around their roots.

Although it was a poncho, it was not made of nylon; instead, it was some kind of indescribable *GGO*-unique futuristic material.

It was so light that you could forget you were wearing it, and it moved seamlessly, so there was no flapping and crinkling. And if you spent some extra money, you could get them with special chameleonlike abilities that allowed you to change their camo patterns automatically or fool night-vision goggles. Pitohui had all those options enabled, naturally. There was no reason for her not to. *I'm a hit singer in real life. I got money.*

When she had it pulled over her head, it hid her KTR-09 assault rifle. She began to examine the area.

The large trees grew at intervals of about ten yards. She glanced from tree to tree in the mist, searching for something.

"Found it."

Finally, about fifteen yards away, she approached a particular tree. It had a similar look and height as the other trees and was nearly ten feet wide, but there was one feature that set it apart.

At the base of its trunk, there was a very large hole, about five feet tall and wide and extending nearly seven feet into the trunk itself. In other words, a hollow in the tree.

Pitohui knew these giant trees were created and then reused to cut down on production and design costs when building out map data. Of course, if all the objects you could see were copied and pasted, players would notice. They would complain to the devs.

So every now and then, you'd see an alternate design slip in. Very occasionally and only a few in total number.

For big, huge trees, that would be a specimen with a large hole in the trunk.

Only someone as keenly observant as Pitohui, and with as much time logged in to *GGO*, would remember that.

"There we go!" she said out loud, intentionally trying to draw attention, and sidled into the hollow butt-first.

The Remington M870 Breacher shotgun she kept on her left hip was a bit in the way, so she dematerialized it and its holder, sending it back into her inventory.

Everything else, including the KTR-09, fit snugly under the poncho.

"Ahhh, isn't this pleasant?"

In the real world, the hollow of a tree like this would be damp and clammy, with strange-looking mushrooms in it and tons of bugs with too many legs on them. *GGO*'s draw was its realism, but it didn't go to *that* much trouble.

Inside the tree, you were surrounded by walls of a favorable thickness. It made for a very pleasant hideout for a person to cram inside.

"Ahhh, pleasant. Yes, pleasant, indeed."

Thanks to the camouflage poncho, nobody would see Pitohui inside the hollow unless they really stared into it. Or used a flashlight.

And if they did, they would get skewered through the throat or brain with a photon sword the very next instant.

It was okay that she'd lent Llenn two of her swords, because Pitohui had three Muramasa F9s, in fact. She'd bought the extra just before SJ5. As she'd said earlier, she got money.

So after 1:10, she lazily closed her eyes and spent her time mostly napping, until Thane's alliance woke her up.

First she heard voices in the distance calling for more players, and later, footsteps much closer.

She decided to keep an eye out because she didn't have much else of a choice, but as it happened, she was quite fortunate.

Two of the players drawn by Thane's summons happened to pass right beside her hideout tree. Though she couldn't see them, she could tell that they recognized each other in the mist.

"You teaming up with the commentator guy? Guess we're on a cease-fire, then."

"Okay, sure. I want that hundred million, too. No point in killing each other here."

They began to walk in the same direction shoulder to shoulder.

Right through the narrow view the hole in the tree offered her, she could see the two players walking away.

Here's my chance.

Pitohui slithered into motion.

She kept her distance, careful not to lose sight of them in the mist as well as avoiding the presence of any other players behind her. And just when the meetup of Thane's party was barely visible, she stopped to eavesdrop on their conversation.

Now, ten-plus minutes later, she was back in her cozy tree hole, listening to the distant sounds of gunfire until it abruptly stopped.

"Ah. I think Llenn and Fuka killed them all."

She had no doubt at all in her teammates' victory.

The clock said it was 1:50.

✳   ✳   ✳

At 1:10, Shirley started off her game on a firm, packed field of snow that looked like a flat white desert.

"Well…time to kill."

As she'd stated over the comm, she wore galoshes with skis attached to the soles. These were cross-country skis people used for hunting in the real world.

There was sealskin on the underside of the skis, so they were very smooth going forward but almost never slid backward. That meant you could alternate your feet and just keep sliding up a slope without worrying about traction.

They'd played a big part in her plan to mess up Pitohui in SJ2, and in the recent Five Ordeals, they'd made it possible for her to do the honor of knocking down the building in the snow on a suicide charge.

She also wore a mottled snowy camo poncho of white and gray, much like Llenn's.

Her favorite sniper rifle, the R93 Tactical 2, swung in front of her body and poncho on a longer sling that ran behind her neck and right shoulder. She kept the muzzle low and the grip just in front of her right flank.

It would be easier to move around with it slung over her back, but this way made it much easier to react and shoot on short notice. She could lift it up, press the stock to her shoulder, and fire, all in one smooth motion.

Of course, she'd loaded her special killer explosive bullets, which detonated on impact. There was one in the chamber and five in the magazine.

As a licensed gun owner, she always wanted to keep the safety on—but this was combat, not hunting, and a game, not real life. So she kept it off.

There was one other difference between how she handled guns in *GGO* and in real life: whether she placed tape on the muzzle.

Shirley's real-life identity, Mai Kirishima, primarily hunted in the snow. Setting aside hunts of Yezo sika deer in the summer for overpopulation, the hunts during the winter almost always took place in a snowy setting.

The R93 Tactical 2 that she took hunting, which she'd earned the license to carry and use, always had tape over the muzzle. She used masking tape so that she could tear it easily. The wide strip would completely cover the opening at the end of the barrel.

This was to prevent any foreign objects from getting inside the gun. That could mean dirt but usually meant snow. When you were hiking through the snow in the forest, snow falling off branches onto you was a very common occurrence.

If it fell on your head, no harm, no foul. But if you were carrying your rifle with the barrel pointed straight up, the results could be disastrous. And if you carried the gun pointed downward, the tip would invariably get dragged through the snow, which would have the same effect.

A little bit of soft snow in the barrel probably wouldn't have an effect on firing. But if it melted inside and froze again into ice, you had a major problem.

Foreign material inside the barrel had a negative effect on accuracy, and at worst, it could increase the internal pressure enough to rupture the barrel when fired.

Hence the tape. You had to put masking tape over the muzzle, nice and firm.

What do you do when shooting? Rip it off each time?

No. When you see your prey in the mountains, you have to take aim and shoot right away before it escapes. So you shoot through the tape.

When a bullet and its accompanying gas come through the barrel, the tape might as well not even be there. Shooting the gun blows the tape right off, and it has no effect on the accuracy of the shot.

If there's a problem with this method, it's that recovering the tape is almost impossible, so every time you shoot, you're creating litter out in the majesty of nature.

Of course, after firing, it needed to be applied again. So she always kept a roll of masking tape in her pocket.

Around the time they started playing *GGO*, Shirley and her friends in the Kita no Kuni Hunter's Club had a serious debate over whether they should continue their taping practice within the game.

In the end, they came to a very simple conclusion.

"It's such a pain in the ass."

Diversion over.

Shirley held her stock with both hands and asked herself, "Now, which way do I go?"

And just like that, she started running.

The direction didn't really matter to her.

No matter which way she ran, there would be someone, some enemy.

She'd make good use of her skis for quick mobility, and when she saw someone, she'd shoot them and put them away. There was nothing else for her to do at this point in time.

The area was covered in thick fog, and there was snow underfoot. Everything she could see was white and plodding, but Shirley moved for all she was worth.

Naturally, the skis made it much easier than running on her feet alone. The ground moved past her at a comfortable rate—*swish, swish, swish.*

There was one other feature of skis that spelled disaster for her foes in this scenario.

Ah, there's one.

It was that they were much quieter than running.

He never noticed the faint sound of friction before he died.

It took Shirley only three hundred yards of distance from her starting point to find another player.

He was wearing very visible dark-green camo on the snowy background and showed no sign of turning around to see her. It was hard to know what he was doing, other than just standing there.

Shirley lifted the R93 Tactical 2 as she skied along and pointed the very large muzzle break at him.

The running snapshot—firing while on the move—was Shirley's forte. And the target was only about fifty feet away. It would be hard to miss at that distance. If this were a tabletop RPG, she would've hit him without even needing to roll a die.

There was the crack of the gunshot, and the man took an exploding round to the back. The resulting shock wave from the explosion hurled him forward.

She didn't even wait to see the DEAD tag, yanking the straight-pull bolt back and forth to load the next shot and continuing on her way.

She already knew full well that SJ5's map was not going to be covered entirely in snow. Based on previous Squad Jams, each setting was going to cover only about a quarter of the overall map in total.

In other words, if the entire map was exactly ten miles to a side, each sector would be five square miles to a side. If she kept rushing about at this speed, she would reach the end of it before long.

But if that happened and the terrain was changing, Shirley could just stop, switch directions, and then race to the next borderline.

She would travel as far through the snow as she could and eliminate as many enemies as she could.

It was the greatest manhunt she could imagine, making the fullest use of her unique skills.

"Ha-ha-ha!" Shirley chuckled. Her legs moved ceaselessly. "*GGO* is so damn fun!"

It was 1:19 when Shirley found it.

She had shot and killed three players on sight so far. The next

scan was imminent, so she was thinking she should stop moving on the skis, flatten herself against the snow, and watch the scan.

"There."

On the left side in the direction she was heading, a dark shape appeared through the mist and vanished just as quickly.

In other words, Shirley had approached the figure at a diagonal and passed them. The encounter was just at the limit of visibility and lasted a fraction of a second.

If the enemy noticed her, too, they would come after her.

Shirley slowed on the skis, crouched down, and glared at the direction the shadow had vanished.

At the very least, if she stayed crouched, she'd be able to spot whoever might be coming first. If she could get off the first shot, she was guaranteed to win.

She waited ten very tense seconds, but there was no response.

In that case...

Shirley decided she would do the chasing instead.

She stood up, glancing around at her surroundings, and began to slowly move in the direction she'd seen the figure, striding silently on the skis and being careful not to make any extra noise.

She kept the R93 Tactical 2 pressed against her shoulder, but eventually decided to lower it a little. The instant she determined her target could be shot, she'd only need to lift the gun a little, peer through the scope, and fire. If the enemy noticed her at the same time, she'd flop forward to make a smaller window before she shot.

Shirley slid, foot after foot, through the snow and gave up on watching the second scan roll in.

More important was her target.

She would shoot them, dispatch them—but not rip out their entrails or cut off their head or anything like that.

There!

She saw it: the black shadow. Calculating from the depth of the fog, she estimated the distance at about twenty yards.

Shirley stopped to watch the shadow's movement. If it got

fainter, it was moving away. If it got sharper, it was coming her way.

There was no movement.

The shadow remained where it was, exactly as thick as it was. For a moment, she wondered if it wasn't even a person at all but a tree stump or something of that nature. But the chances were low.

Then Shirley spotted a glowing white spot at the edge of the shadow, and at last she understood.

They're watching the scan! she realized. That left just one choice of action.

She craned her neck to find the right angle where the light from the scanner's screen was not visible behind the shadow—the angle that would let her approach from directly behind them.

She also turned left and right to confirm that no other enemies were nearby. She didn't want to be so focused on her prey that she wound up someone else's prey instead.

Even in real life, it was possible to be so intent on a Yezo sika deer that you failed to notice a bear approaching from behind. And if anything, the players in *GGO* were more ruthless and dangerous than that.

There were no enemies around.

All I have to do is take them out. Shirley snuck forward. Toward the shadow.

Carefully, sneakily, she approached, with the muzzle of her gun trained right at the figure.

If she shot now, she could hit their back and finish off the target.

But Shirley did not do that.

"......"

Even she did not know why.

Her finger had been reaching for the trigger, but she silently straightened it out.

She decided to get closer, shifting her feet to move farther forward.

The figure was utterly still and silent before her.

"!"

And then she properly saw him.

A man standing carelessly in the midst of the snow, gazing intently at the Satellite Scan terminal in his left hand, tapping relentlessly on the screen with his right.

She could make out all the details.

On his back was an enormous backpack that rivaled even M's majestic example.

Over the curve of the pack, she could just faintly make out his head, which was covered by a helmet that looked like it belonged to a tinplate robot.

His busy hand and his stock-still legs were covered by similarly robotic armor.

He's from that suicide-bombing team!

All of Shirley's hair stood on end. Virtually speaking, of course.

She froze about thirty feet away, long gun pointed right at him.

If I'd shot at him a moment ago...

The bullet would have hit the backpack.

The high-performance explosives carried in his backpack did not act like plasma grenades. A normal bullet would only punch a funny hole in the explosive and would not start a chain reaction explosion.

But what if it weren't a regular bullet, but one of Shirley's special explosive rounds? Then it would have set off the bomb.

So if she had fired, she would have been blasted to smithereens and right out of SJ5 in the very next instant.

"......"

Shirley decided that she was now willing to believe in a sixth sense. In the virtual world, at least.

It was probably her grandmother who had saved her life just now.

"I don't know how I feel about girls killing things," she had said, expressing her reservations about Shirley becoming a hunter.

And then, after the first time Shirley cooked her a stew of Yezo sika venison, that same grandmother sent her a text message later, asking, WHEN'S THE NEXT TIME YOU'RE GOING HUNTING, MAI?

Her grandmother was still alive and well, by the way.

*   *   *

Well, what am I supposed to do now? Shirley wondered.

The bomber was absorbed in his Satellite Scanner, a shocking lack of caution for any Squad Jam participant. But there was no guarantee he wouldn't spin around the next moment, and then Shirley would have no choice but to shoot.

However, he had armor on the front side that was meant to help him survive to get closer to the target of his bombing run. In the battle on the bridge in SJ4, Shirley had used an explosive round on her pursuer's thigh, making him fall to the ground.

That had successfully gotten him to self-destruct where he was, saving the rest of the team—but she hadn't been sure if she'd successfully shot through his armor plating at the time. Even on the replay, it was hard to tell.

According to M, their armor couldn't be as tough as his shield or the expensive full-body armor that T-S spent so much cash on. But could she kill him instantly with a headshot using her explosive round?

If it wasn't an insta-kill and it gave him even a single second before he died, he would manage to self-destruct. He just had to pull the string coming from his backpack.

If he were going to die and lose SJ5, he would want to at least blow up and take out someone else with him. It's what she would do if she were him.

Should I pull back? she thought, but that, too, was a risk.

Her cross-country skis could not simply slide backward like regular skis.

To leave this location, she would have to lift her feet in sequence until she had completed a one-eighty turn, jump to perform a quick aerial about-face, or proceed forward and curve away from the hostile target.

Each option would take time and had the risk of making sound. If he noticed her, she'd be attacked from behind.

The man presumably had some kind of firearm. Perhaps something light and compact, like a submachine gun. Or even just a pistol.

He certainly wouldn't have come to a ferocious, intense battlefield with an idiotic loadout like nothing but heavy explosives, after all.

In fact, he *did* have that exact idiotic loadout, but Shirley didn't know that. She couldn't be expected to know that.

Shit...I'm really slipping, Shirley swore at herself.

She'd gotten too close. But she wouldn't have noticed the details of his identity if she hadn't approached. Damned if you do and damned if you don't.

If she crouched down, would he simply walk away without noticing her?

Her chances would be better, but she didn't want to bet her life on something like that.

And thus in the end, by pure elimination, there is just one option.

Shirley made a haiku in her mind. With one extra syllable.

She took another step closer.

*   *   *

At 1:12, while her partner was away enjoying *GGO*, Squad Jam, and the pure act of killing to her heart's content, Clarence was feeling more than a little freaked out and weak-willed.

"Man, I'm so lonely..."

She had told M, "Okay! I'll just enjoy myself, then. It's not like I'm carrying anyone else's stuff. If I die, big whoop!" but that had been empty cheer. It was a bluff, and now she could admit it.

Being all alone in thick mist wasn't lonely? How could it not be?

"And where am I supposed to hide...?"

As M had said, she was surrounded by wasteland.

It was rough, arid desert, with nothing man-made in sight. Under her feet was sand, gravel, and rocks, and each step brought up a little cloud of dust. The ground was essentially flat.

There were rocks scattered around, the smallest going only up to her knee, with the biggest being taller than her. The ones close-up were easy to identify as rocks, but the farther away they got, the more they blended in with the milky-white fog.

The details faded away until they were nothing but a vague, soft silhouette, at which point it became very hard to tell if a shape was a rock or a person.

"I don't like this place," Clarence muttered, squeezing the grip of her AR-57, a curious gun that placed the P90's system inside an AR assault rifle. "But there's no use just standing around daydreaming."

She began to move.

M had instructed them to act slowly, but in this environment with this visibility, going slow and careful was mentally draining.

So she decided not to follow his rules. Nobody was watching her.

Clarence was pretty quick on her feet, if not as fast as Llenn.

"Hi-yah!"

She started off at a dead sprint. At least until she came to a large boulder that was just barely visible.

And once she was clinging to that giant piece of cover that would protect her from attacks, she surveyed the area around her.

She was looking to see if there were any other players nearby, but all she felt was terrified of how all the rocks looked like people.

There's one!

She raised her AR-57 and pointed it, only to find that it was just an unmoving rock.

"Ugh, geez…"

She launched into another sprint for the next large rock she could see. Then she put her back to it, looked around, and ran to the next rock.

Clarence had no idea which way she was going; for all she knew, she could have been going in a circle. Maybe she'd look down at some point and see her own footprints from earlier.

But still, she ran.

"Someone be there, at least. Then I can kill you," she muttered dramatically.

She spent the next four minutes wandering the wasteland in this manner. Then, when surveying the area near the latest rock she reached, she saw a flickering shadow in the mist.

At first she assumed it was just another rock, but then she realized that it was still moving.

"Eep!"

She hid behind the rock and peered around it at the shadow.

From the shadow's point of view, Clarence was one with the rock. So as long as she didn't make any drastic movements, the other person would not notice her.

Just in case, she glanced in the opposite direction to make sure there were no other people moving on that side.

Then Clarence slowly peered around the side to stare at the flickering shadow.

The mist made it impossible to see the finer details. So the shadow wasn't coming into focus, but they also weren't going away. They seemed to be moving from the right to the left, almost entirely parallel with the ground.

Just in case someone else happened to be following the shadow—in other words, if he or she had a traveling companion— she checked the direction that the shadow had come from, but there was no one else.

The figure was moving farther and farther to the left. At this rate, they would be gone before long. They were already going out of sight.

Clarence had a set of options to choose from.

Number one!

I can aim at them now, so shoot! Kill!

The distance was probably about sixty to seventy-five feet. If she took aim with her rifle and shot at full auto, she could probably take out her target.

But what about the low possibility that the shadow could belong to one of her teammates? Or some member of SHINC, who was allied with the team?

Shooting without confirmation was a bit of a problem. Of course, the chances that it was an enemy she could and *should* shoot were much higher.

Number two!

Let them go!

They didn't see her, so it was a valid strategic choice to let them walk away unaware. The target was going to pass out of sight within a few seconds. As long as she traveled in the direction the shadow had come from, she was guaranteed to be safe.

Number three!

Talk to them! "Hello, hello! How are you? Wanna play, mister?"

That was a valid strategy. Whomever the person was, she could suggest a temporary team-up. But that was a risky ploy, because if the other person didn't want to do it, they might immediately shoot her dead.

Number four!

Talk to them, pretend to want to fight together, then when they're caught slipping, do a sneak attack!

That was a fun strategy, one that was sure to feature a very shocked facial expression to look forward to.

She loved that kind of stuff. Clarence was Clarence, after all.

But there was risk involved. She might speak up and immediately get a response of "I don't need partners!" and get shot up.

If you're going to kill them, it's more reliable to just shoot them right from the start.

So what now? Clarence considered her options. She didn't have time.

A second later, she made her decision.

Number five!

I'll do something that's "none of the above"! It'll probably be more fun!

Clarence was indeed Clarence.

Without considering the consequences, she looked for—and found—a large rock near her feet. It was the perfect throwing rock, about the size of a fist and nicely shaped.

She moved the AR-57 to her left hand, picked up the rock, and hurled it with all her strength.

"Hi-yah!"

She'd had plenty of practice throwing in *GGO*, so she was good at it. Yes, from grenades.

She didn't "throw like a girl," or "fail to put her shoulder into it," or anything like that.

The rock hurtled fifty feet or so through the air.

Whud!

"Aaagh!"

Huh?

She actually hit the man where he stood—his yelp confirmed it. Right in the head.

It wasn't her intention. She just thought it would be funny to see him freak out if a rock landed near his feet, and she could play it by ear after that...

"What the—? Huh?!"

The shadow was clearly freaked out and flustered. The smartest move at the moment would be to flee, but he wasn't even doing that.

"I-is someone out there?!"

He was probably pointing his gun in all directions.

Since his reaction was so funny, Clarence crouched again, found another rock, and hurled it the same way.

She did not manage to coincidentally hit him twice. Instead, it made a loud thud close by.

"Eep!" he shrieked, terrified.

Yes, let's freak him out some more, Clarence decided. Because it was fun.

What else could she do at this very moment that would freak him out even more than he already was? Her brain went into overdrive, but shooting him was against the rules. That would kill him, and that wasn't scaring him.

Should I strip to my underwear and make a move on him?

Clarence had attempted this seduction technique in SJ4, and it had worked like gangbusters.

Her body was just an avatar in a virtual world, so she didn't care how much of it people saw—or even touched, if it came to that.

This was a place where you could enjoy things you couldn't do in the real world, like engaging in slaughter and death matches, so in her personal opinion, Clarence thought that people who said getting frisky should be off-limits were off their rockers.

But she declined to execute Operation Underwear.

She'd have to put away the AR-57, and she didn't want to get shot and killed. Plus, it was going to delight the guy. That was wrong. That was the opposite of what she wanted.

So what was the plan?

Bing.

A light bulb flickered on in Clarence's mind.

She also had a stray thought: *Why is the light bulb you see when people get ideas always just a single, bare bulb floating in space? Why isn't it connected to a socket? It's not being powered. It can't possibly turn on that way.*

But the thought had nothing to do with *GGO* or Squad Jam, so she decided to push it out of her head for now.

Back to her moment of inspiration. Pitohui had given her an item, something she might be able to take advantage of here.

Pitohui had used it gleefully at their meetup the other day, and when Clarence showed interest in it, Pitohui had given it to her as casually as if it were a piece of candy.

Clarence waved her hand and brought the item out in order to use it.

Honk-honk!

The wasteland's silence was broken by a raucous trumpet.

In her left hand was a rubber honker, the kind that made a trumpet noise when you squeezed the rubber bulb. It was more accurately known as a bulb horn. In other words, the thing Pito-hui had used in the bar.

"Eep?" the man shrieked, startled by the sudden noise. "Aaaah!"

Then there was gunfire. He had started shooting wildly, aiming at nothing, simply trying to dampen his terror.

But the muzzle did swing in Clarence's direction.

"Yikes!"

She ducked behind the boulder, which trembled as it took a few bullets. With her back against the rock, she saw bullet lines running wildly from behind her to the distance ahead of her. The bullets erased them faster than the speed of sound.

He shot and shot and shot…for about three seconds.

That was probably when he had used up the thirty bullets in his rifle's magazine. The world was suddenly quiet again.

Honk-honk-honk-honk-honk! Honk-honk-honk-honk-honk!

Clarence fired back. It was a rubber horn spray. She was liberal in her application of honks.

"Aaaah! What the hell, man?!"

The man finished reloading and resumed his gunfire. Based on the location of his bullet lines, Clarence knew she wasn't going to get shot, so she kept up with him.

Honk-honk-honk-honk-honk-honk-honk-honk-honk-honk-honk-honk-honk-honk-honk-honk!!

For as long as her wrist strength held out, she tried to match his gunfire with honks. The world of mist was colored with a raucous medley of gunshots and rubber horn honks. It was, frankly, rather insane.

And then all was quiet again.

The gunshots stopped after two seconds.

Honk-honk.

It stopped so suddenly that Clarence hit the horn two more times before noticing.

"Huh?"

She leaned out to take a look and noticed that hanging in the air in the direction where the man had been was now a shining DEAD marker. The fog did not stop it from being clearly visible.

Assuming he hadn't given up in despair on the world and killed himself, or fumbled the gun and accidentally shot himself in the head, that would mean someone else shot him and that another enemy was nearby.

"Oh, crap."

Clarence tossed aside the borrowed horn and gripped her AR-57 with both hands. The horn thudded carelessly to the ground. She had to apologize and tell it that she'd retrieve it with her item window later.

More important was the enemy.

Clarence hunched down behind the rock, preparing herself to fire mercilessly at whoever had shot the man if they came toward her...

"Here we go."

Through the mist, she saw a small shape waver into being, right next to the DEAD tag.

The person was running her way at considerable speed, their silhouette taking shape rapidly as they approached.

"Oh! Ah...um...hey! You! Uhhh..."

Clarence recognized something and hurled not bullets, but her voice.

"Your name! Um, oh yeah! Tanya!"

She swerved around the side of the boulder and called the player's name...

Shunk!

...right as Tanya, startled, fired a shot from her silenced Bizon submachine gun.

"Ughhhh, I'll never forget this... I'll curse you to your grandchildren's grandchildren's generationnnn..."

"I'm so sorry. I really mean it."

"Eh, it's fine. Today is No Worries Day."

Clarence, with her black gear and black hair, and Tanya, with white hair and speckled green camo, sat at the foot of the large boulder, watching opposite directions.

There was still a bright-red damage mark on Clarence's cheek from where she got shot.

About thirty seconds earlier, Tanya's accidental 9 mm Parabellum bullet flew with unerring accuracy at Clarence, hit her smack on the right cheek, and passed through her left.

"Gblag!"

Clarence lost a third of her overall hit points. But if it had struck her just four inches to the side, it would have gone through her cerebellum and killed her instantly, so in a sense, she was lucky.

"Hyaaaa! I'm sorry, I'm sorry, I'm sorryyy!"

Tanya lowered her gun and bowed frantically. She knew she had just shot a friend.

Clarence took a med kit immediately to start the healing process.

For now, they decided to stay put, hold their backs to the rock, and use all four eyes to monitor the surrounding area. If any enemies approached, they would fight them off together.

"In any case, now we have twice the eyes! That's way, way more reliable than just wandering around alone!" Clarence murmured quietly but happily. She wasn't just saying that; it was her honest opinion.

Since they were hooked up via the comm, Tanya heard every word.

"Yes, I agree! Also, I just have to say, this new rule that the team has to get split up like this…"

"*Totally sucks!*" they agreed in unison.

The two girls chuckled over their little moment. It was like something out of a school classroom. A refreshing, pleasant scene within the general misery of *GGO*.

But the man was already dead, so there was no else around to enjoy the moment. Too bad.

"I bet our team leader, Llenn, is having a terrible time," Clarence murmured.

There was no X mark on the list of teammates in the upper left of her vision, so she knew Llenn was still alive, but that was the extent of the information; she could be heavily injured, for all they knew.

"How about your Boss?" Clarence asked.

To her surprise, Tanya replied, "Oh, SHINC's team leader isn't Boss this time."

"No way!"

"It's Anna. We thought we might use the leader position as a decoy trap. But we weren't expecting these special rules. Anna's probably feeling so lonely with everyone going after her... I hope she isn't crying."

"She's the blonde one with the sunglasses, right? She'll be fine; she's pretty. I bet she'll have all the men around her eating out of her hand. And then she'll cut off their heads while they're bending over."

"Ha-ha-ha."

They continued chatting like this, waiting for enemies to arrive, but no one did. Instead, the only thing that arrived was the scan at 1:20. It was the second of the day.

"But you know," Tanya remarked, "there's kind of no point to watching the scan, because there's at least a hundred players wandering all over the place who won't show up on it."

She was right. Just because the scan didn't show any dots near you didn't mean you were safe.

But at the same time, your own location wasn't going to show up, so it didn't mean anyone was coming for you, either.

"So it's probably best if we just don't move," Clarence said, right as the clock hit 1:20.

They watched the second Satellite Scan together, eyes roaming ceaselessly between their screens and the space around them. They didn't forget to keep the scanners hidden against their bodies to prevent the light from showing.

Not a single one of the teams had been fully eliminated.

"Anna seems to have come a little closer to our location. We're around the middle of the map," Tanya noted. They had a general idea of their location now.

Since Clarence had run here and there, and Tanya had stayed on the move, the combination of their map data gave their auto-mapped area a notable increase in size. This change helped give them a good idea of where on the square field map they were located.

The center of the screen was where the map had been revealed. Anna, who had started all the way in the upper right (northeast) corner, had moved her way a bit closer to them in the middle.

"But she's still at least a mile and a half away... That's a really long distance to travel safely in the middle of this mist... since there are probably tons of enemies along the way," Tanya explained.

"Should we go to her instead?" Clarence suggested.

But Tanya wasn't convinced. "The thing is, Boss said that if you're in a safe place, there's no reason to risk danger to go any-where. Although I *did* come over here because I heard the gunshots, so what do I know?"

"Uh-huh. I guess it would be best to just chill here for an hour, then?" Clarence wondered, sliding the Satellite Scanner back into her pants pocket now that its purpose had been served.

"Enemy!" Tanya hissed.

When Tanya came rolling over toward her, Clarence under-stood that someone had approached through the mist from Tanya's side. She raised her AR-57, stood in a half crouch, and peered carefully around the edge of the rock.

There was a man rushing through the mist.

"It's the optical team," Tanya hissed.

He was holding an MG 2504, a machine-gun-type optical gun. Since it was clearly not a real-life gun, it was obvious that he was a member of RGB, the team that was infamous for always using optical guns. They were the only ones who did that in Squad Jam, in which optical guns were largely useless because they were unsuited for PvP combat. It was just their thing.

Shots from optical guns were weakened by the optical defensive fields that everyone carried with them, so they didn't do a ton of damage, but the range was close, and the machine-gun type could be annoying because they fired so fast. It wouldn't do to be careless.

Clarence was wondering what they ought to do when she noticed something about him.

"Wait, is he being chased?"

The man in the mist seemed to be backing away from someone, looking over his shoulder occasionally. So his gun was pointed away, and he had his back toward the girls.

"Yeah, he's running away."

The man eventually turned around to run in earnest. He rushed behind a rock to hide. It was about fifteen yards away from Clarence and Tanya.

With where he was hiding, over on their right side, he was actually exposing his left side to the two girls.

"He's going to be a problem if he's hanging out just over there," Clarence murmured.

"Yeah. Should I shoot him?" Tanya suggested.

"I wanna shoot him, too."

"Yeah, but my gun's got the silencer on it."

"I have a slight boost in damage, so mine is better."

The two girls were bro-ing out and having a dick-measuring contest. It was really something.

"Okay, then! Let's just have fun killing the target together," Clarence offered, right as the RGB man started shooting. An optical gun was lighter than a live-ammo gun, so even as a bulky machine gun, he could quickly lift it to his shoulder to fire.

He steadied the MG 2504 and opened furious automatic fire while hiding behind the rock. It made a unique optical firing sound—*pyew-pyew-pyew-pyew-pyew-pyew*—and sprayed yellow projectiles toward the left, from Clarence and Tanya's line of sight.

Optical guns could be customized to fire in either Power Mode or Firing Mode.

In Power Mode, the rate of fire was lower, but each shot carried a heavier punch, and Firing Mode was the opposite.

He had his gun on Firing Mode. He continued shooting, spraying the area with a wide array of shots rather than focusing on a single point. The rate of fire was so high that it looked like he was spraying a hose.

The lines of optical bullets snaked and curved like whips as they vanished into the mist, but the girls couldn't see his enemy. Was he seeing someone?

After ten seconds of fierce optical blasting, everything went quiet at last.

"Did he get it done?"

"You think?"

Tanya's and Clarence's questions were emphatically answered with a furious volley of return fire.

Duh-duh-duh-duh-duh-duh-duh-duh-duh.

It was deep and impactful, shaking the ground beneath their feet.

There was a good three seconds of this new, heavy gunfire, which made the optical gun sound like a child's toy.

The bullets struck the rock the RGB man was hiding behind, gouging out chunks and chips of the boulder.

Tanya and Clarence found their gazes drawn from the man being shot at to the direction of his shooter. Through the haze of the distant mist was the bright and unmistakable light of a muzzle flash, along with the shape of the man holding it.

He was tall and well-muscled, with his brown hair slicked back like a rooster's comb. He wore a green fleece jacket and black combat pants, with a large M240B machine gun pressed to his shoulder.

The large box on his back was a backpack-style ammo loading system.

It was Huey, one of the members of ZEMAL.

Huey was lashing the rock at a pace of ten 7.62 mm rounds per second. They blasted the rock, spraying chips of stone.

"Aaah!"

The unfortunate man was caught in the blast zone, red damage effects glowing all over his body and turning him into a big red doll. The DEAD tag popped into existence above his body.

Taking his finger off the trigger, he stopped walking. He seemed to be listening and watching the area carefully.

A wild ZEMAL appeared!

What now?

"Run!"

Tanya and Clarence spoke in unison. It was a unanimous decision.

They couldn't take on a juggernaut of pure firepower like him. The instant they took a dinky little potshot at him, he would blast them to bits under a hail of bullets. Like he'd done to the man just now, he would simply tunnel through any rock they tried to hide behind.

If they attempted to jump him from two directions in a pincer attack, one of them might survive the encounter, but that wasn't going to help their team. The point of this event was to be the champions.

When the only good outcome is a tie, then, as a wise man once said: Of the Thirty-Six Stratagems, retreat is best.

The two girls turned on their heels and began to run. The big rock should have been hiding them from Huey's line of sight, but they sprinted all the same.

"Don't come after us!"

"Stay away!"

It was a wild sprint throwing caution to the wind, with no thought for their course.

And somehow, they didn't get spotted.

There was no chasing fire from Huey as they ran.

Even still, they charged pell-mell for safety.

"Where are we running?"

"I don't know!"

"Let's go as far as we can, then!"

"Sounds good!"

They ran with a wild, carefree euphoria, like the fabled runner's high. Tanya was the faster of the two, but because of the poor visibility, she held back on her speed, which put her at the same pace as Clarence.

They were shoulder to shoulder.

"Ah-ha-ha, this is fun!" remarked Clarence, her white teeth sparkling.

"Yeah, it's great!" Tanya beamed.

"What's that?" muttered a player who spotted the two girls running through the mist, but because of the distance and angle, they lost sight of them. It seemed that luck was their running companion.

"The fun part about VR games is that you can really test your physical limits!" said Tanya, who'd started using full-dive gear for the sake of her gymnastics team.

"I get that! It's really fun being able to do things you can't do in real life!" agreed Clarence at a full sprint. The meaning of those words was slightly different in each girl's head, but neither of them realized it.

Wistfully, Clarence added, "If only I could live on this side... forever. I don't think...I like reality very much... Still hate it..."

Tanya had no response to this.

They ran together for three minutes, at which point they came to a stop.

"Hmm?"

"Wha—?"

There was a wall approaching through the fog.

First there was something black jutting upward beyond the veil of milky white, and then it approached them with shocking speed—in total silence.

In reality, they were the ones who were running, so when they stopped in alarm, the obstacle stopped as well.

"What is this...?" Tanya murmured.

"A wall?"

Clarence approached the object slowly, and when it was close enough to make out the details, she looked up.

What she saw was a huge, European-style castle wall, built of light-brown stone. Because of the mist, it was impossible to make out the top or the sides in either direction.

All she could tell was that it was really, really tall and really, really wide.

There were letters on the wall's surface.

"Oh?"

"Ah!"

To Tanya's and Clarence's shock, letters about three times the size of a person rose to visibility, as though they were made with invisible ink being exposed to the light.

In other words, the letters were designed to provide information if a player came to them.

Soon the letters were fully formed and combined into a sentence.

"Oh my...," said Tanya, reading them.

"Oh my...," said Clarence, shocked.

Clarence looked at Tanya and asked the first question that came to mind.

"Why is it in the generic Mincho font?"

"Really?" Tanya replied. "*That's* your question?"

CHAPTER 8

What M Did

SECT.8

CHAPTER 8
What M Did

"Well..."

M met the 1:10 marker while on the ground floor of a building. His starting point was in a city.

The abandoned city biome was a common one in *GGO*, as seen previously in SJ1 and SJ4.

The thick fog covering everything gave him little visibility, but based on what he could see, it was fairly easy to predict.

There would be a cross pattern of streets like a classic American city, with imposing buildings dropped onto each block between the intersections. At their biggest, a single structure could occupy the entire block. On the smaller side, it could be several buildings.

The empty buildings were plain and geometric. The shorter ones were about ten stories, while the tallest went up to thirty or so.

And every now and then, you saw an example of a building with an especially elaborate design that an artist really wanted to create—and nobody bothered to stop them from doing it.

Others looked like they'd had their budget accidentally allocated to an extra digit and stood over seven hundred feet tall, like chimneys towering over all.

M started the game on one of the major roads passing through this city, so he immediately took refuge in the nearest building.

He was probably invisible thanks to the mist, but he did so just in case.

Any fight here would inevitably be an urban battle. In *GGO*, as in the real world, urban battles involved many places to hide and thus often became close-range altercations that could be extremely intense.

And his enemies could very well be in the next building over. Or even in the next room over.

Each street and building was a territory to fight over. You'd have to shoot at any enemy you saw, toss a grenade, or resort to hand-to-hand combat. Urban combat was a nasty, violent phenomenon. It was a good thing this was a game.

But for M, this ruined city was the perfect place to hide until two o'clock. There were any number of hiding places. It was much easier on the mind than Clarence's situation, that was certain.

Bold action was meaningless until two o'clock, when the mist was clear. Best just to find a hiding spot and hunker down.

He made his way through the rubble of the building, occasionally moving it out of the way in his search for a staircase. Soon he found it, and quietly climbed the steps, watching his footing.

His gun was the M14 EBR, a 7.62 mm sniper rifle accurate to eight hundred yards. Although he would be hiding, it would be useful for shooting at the road from a high point.

On the downside, if someone knew he was here, they could wait on the first floor, making it much harder for him to escape the building. But only if that enemy was working with a team. In this case, ease of sniping would win out.

M's considerable size moved quietly up the darkened stairs.

Ruins in *GGO* sometimes surprised the player with crumbling step traps, so he took his time, carefully testing each step before he put his full weight on it.

On a landing, he saw a sign on the wall that indicated in fading writing that the building had about twenty floors.

M finished his ascent at the fifth floor and made his way through an office area, careful that he didn't fall through any weak spots in the hallway. Soon he reached the exterior wall of the building, offering him a view of the street.

He approached the window, which ran from ceiling to floor with the glass blown out, and stopped short. Next, he materialized a small mirror.

It was a rounded convex mirror, like a smaller version of the blind-curve mirrors placed on roads.

By looking through a mirror like this, he could keep his back to the tough, protective wall and see the street below from considerably higher safety.

While it was faded by mist, he could indeed make out the ground, just barely.

The street was very wide, perhaps a hundred feet across. There were three lanes in each direction, six in total. Even the sidewalks were built to be very spacious.

The concrete here was relatively intact, with a flat enough surface that cars could ostensibly ride over it. But there were no cars on the road. No burned-out wrecks or usable cars, at least within the range of what he could see.

It was just a clear, fairly nice stretch of road.

"Interesting…," he murmured, having recognized something.

But none of his teammates were around, so there was no one to ask him what he noticed.

He glanced at his wristwatch: 1:14.

And from this point on, let's just watch and wait.

Here you'll see M, watching and waiting.

His body was as large as a boulder and, for the time being, as still as a boulder, too.

M, or more accurately the player controlling him, Goushi Asougi, was used to waiting.

He was stalwart—a very patient person who would happily wait for hours doing nothing if that was for the sake of his goal.

Soon it was 1:20.

"Let's see."

He took out his Satellite Scanner and placed it inside his bush hat, which he held in front of his face. That was to ensure the light didn't escape.

The scan started up, displaying its results.

Ten minutes ago, the LPFM dot had been at what appeared to be the edge of the map, and it was still around the same spot. He knew from the display of his teammates' names on the left that Llenn wasn't dead, but he had no idea what she was currently doing. Hopefully, something good.

As for his own location, he had done almost no two-dimensional movement, so there was no real mapping done. Even zooming all the way in, he couldn't see very much detail.

He couldn't do anything about that, though. It wasn't wise to run around just to get more map info. M decided to wait in the same location for another ten minutes.

Eight minutes passed.

The universe was utterly silent in that time.

It was frighteningly quiet, in fact.

Every other player in the area had clearly chosen the same strategy. They weren't going to take risks before two o'clock, either.

There were no nearby firefights, no wind, and thus no sound, just time slowly ticking away.

M had plenty of time to himself to think.

He thought about a great many things, in fact.

About his time as Goushi Asougi from birth through college, a dark time of youth that left him unfulfilled and unhappy.

About the goddess he met out of the blue one day.

About his fateful choice to follow his goddess home.

About coincidentally getting beaten to a pulp by his goddess.

About the days of happiness, pain, and fulfillment ever since.

And about the days in which he understood why he'd been born.

About the days he spent in a video game with his goddess, after she claimed she was going to risk her life inside the game.

About when he nearly learned how he was going to die.

About the little thing named Llenn who saved their lives.

And about everything from that point until today.

"Hmm?"

At about 1:28, M heard a faint, distant, but deep noise.

It seemed like the sound of combat in some far-off location, perhaps a grenade explosion in another building, but there was no sound that followed it, and everything went quiet again.

"......"

M silently turned so that he was looking out the window with his own eyes, rather than through the mirror.

The mist-shrouded dead city was just as it had appeared earlier: quiet and foreboding.

"......"

M's craggy rock face and firm rock body returned to their prior position.

A short time later, his wristwatch vibrated.

It was 1:29:30.

At one thirty, everyone's ammo and energy returned in full, but it meant nothing to M, because he hadn't fired a single shot in SJ5.

He used his bush hat to cover the screen once again while he watched the third Satellite Scan.

Llenn had moved farther to the northeast.

He couldn't tell what she was doing from here; he could only hope it was good. Llenn would probably be fine, though.

She was strong; there was no doubt about that. She was the only character whom he and Pitohui really feared.

Similarly, the other corner teams—MMTM, SHINC, and ZEMAL—had moved slightly toward the center. Either they had steadily started creeping toward a meetup or they had reasons they couldn't stay put.

There were thirty other teams. None of them had been fully eliminated yet.

That was about all he learned. The scan was finished.

He was preparing to go into another ten-minute period of Zen meditation.

When...*ta-ta-ta-ta-ta-tat.*

Tight, crisp, percussive gunfire broke the silence from the distance.

Then the sound happened again, but a bit louder, as though a volume knob had been turned from two to four.

Someone was firing a gun on auto. Whether it was combat or a test-fire or a trap meant to lure out foes into the open was unknown.

Because the building walls caused echoing, it was difficult to pin down an exact location, but he could tell generally which direction it was from.

The gunfire was coming from the right side when he faced the street out the window.

Ta-ta-ta-ta-ta-ta-tan, do-doom. Ta-ta-tan, doom. Ta-tan, doom.

It was getting louder, and other types of guns were joining in.

Unless it was one very talented freak shooting two different kinds of gun at the same time, it was now two players firing different guns together.

Based on his ears and brain, M could hazard a guess.

The first, lighter gunfire was probably a 5.56 mm assault rifle. The louder, heavier shots that joined in came from a 7.62 mm battle rifle.

There were other things he could tell just from hearing the sound.

They were not fighting against each other. It was not a firefight. They were firing at the same enemy.

M moved to stand against the wall near the window. But not right up to the edge, where he could be seen from outside. He was well away, about six feet from the actual window. Then he surveyed the area.

He was checking to see if anyone else was hiding inside like he was but had come to the window to see about the noise.

It seemed to be all right. M turned to the direction of the gun-fire, the right side of the street before him.

And then he saw something.

Someone was running down the wide street, visible through the thinning mist. And he could tell right away who it was.

It was a woman with long blond hair wearing Russian-style camo with speckled green dots. She also sported sunglasses and a camo beanie.

It was Anna.

She was the Dragunov-SVD-toting sniper of SHINC, their sister team.

On the inside, she was Moe Annaka, a second-year high school student who looked chill and reserved—and indeed *was* chill and reserved. Goushi had met her at karaoke.

And now she was running desperately down the street.

She was moving down the middle of the wide road, holding her narrow Dragunov in both hands. At times, she threw in a side step in either direction, and she was constantly looking over her shoulder as she sprinted. Her wavy golden hair was trailing behind her.

She'd already taken a number of shots; red spots glowed on her body. The spots on her legs had to hurt pretty badly, but she kept running regardless. The fact that her core was so steady was a testament to her player's innate athletic skill.

Bullet lines and their bullets flew past, chasing after Anna.

M instantly understood the situation.

It would be silly if you couldn't. Anna was being chased by at least two enemies. The end.

Because of the mist, you couldn't see any enemies at least thirty yards away. That was why Anna kept running so hard.

Most likely, the enemy was about as fast, so they were maintaining a distance that just barely gave them a glimpse of her shadow. And their plan was to keep shooting as they ran, hoping they could at least get a coincidental hit on her.

Anna could see the bullet lines, so she kept sidestepping and dodging bullets as she ran.

She did not run into any of the buildings on either side of the street.

If her pursuers saw her do that, she was trapped. They could follow her inside, and then she'd be at an extreme disadvantage. She'd die in battle for sure.

So she was running for all she was worth in the open, hoping to leave her foes behind in the dust—or rather, the mist.

"That was a good call," M said, in the past tense, notably.

He watched her pass right beneath him, set his scope to the lowest zoom level, and lifted his M14 EBR. He was not aiming it yet.

Then he moved over to the far wall and looked down at the street to the right of his position.

His eyes picked up on two men emerging from the mist. Though they were hazy, he could still identify them.

One was in reddish-brown camo and shooting an AC-556F. He was in a team that had been competing ever since SJ1.

The other was a man styled like a Rhodesian Bush War mercenary, holding an FAL assault rifle and wearing a unique camo outfit and chest rig. He was a member of NSS, the historical cosplay team.

With one smooth, speedy motion, M steadied his gun and first placed the scope sights over the man in the reddish-brown camo, who was looking ready to fire.

Because he was running, M aimed a bit ahead of his position. The instant his finger was about to come into contact with the trigger, he tugged it in and pulled.

Bam!

The M14 EBR emitted a short, fierce burst. The loading lever on the right side of the gun cycled violently along with the bolt inside. An empty cartridge shot out of the gun and the next bullet loaded into the chamber, all in a single instant.

The man in the reddish-brown camo was shot through the neck. His neckbones were shattered, putting him on course for an unavoidable death within the next few seconds.

While he fell, still technically alive, M was already aiming at the Rhodesian mercenary to the right.

The second shot emerged in quick order, passing through the man's head from the upper diagonal through the bottom on the other side. He didn't even realize his friend had been shot yet.

Anna heard two shots overhead and noticed that everything went silent after that.

"……"

After a moment's indecision, she stopped running.

If the shooter was an ally, they could team up.

But if it was just another enemy using the opportunity to score some quick kills, then she would be the next target.

Anna looked up at the building on her right.

In a broken windowsill on the fifth floor, she saw a hat and arm waving wildly at her.

It was 1:33.

"Thanks for saving me, Mr. M. I really owe you one," said Anna as soon as she reached the floor where M had camped out.

"That's not necessary. And please, no formal titles. It's just more syllables you'll feel compelled to say out loud when you should be conveying information as quickly as possible. Also, you're welcome, Anna," he replied.

He was keeping his eye on the two bodies with DEAD tags down below and did not turn to face Anna.

Anna crouched just past the entrance to the floor, keeping her eye on the hallway and anyone who might try to come up toward them.

A forty-eight-inch Dragunov was a difficult weapon to use indoors, but her only other weapon was a 9 mm Strizh pistol, so that left her with little choice. She opted for power.

M brought up his game window and requested Anna hook up her comm to his. They were several yards apart, but it was still close enough for the request to go through.

With their earpieces connected, M asked her quietly, "How's the damage?"

"About half; I got shot all over. I used an emergency med kit earlier."

"That was a close one. Glad I was able to save you. I started here. What about you?"

"I was a bit to the northeast, right near the northeast corner of the map. I'm actually the team leader this time. I was staying hidden, but two guys nearby easily spotted me after the scan, and that's why they were chasing me."

"Ahhh, I see..."

He was drawing a map inside his head.

Now he knew that SHINC was placed to start at the opposite corner of LPFM, since Llenn was in the southwest.

Because Anna was placed there, that told him he was somewhere in the northeast quadrant of the map. It also meant that as long as he was with Anna, his location was being revealed, too, every ten minutes when the scan arrived.

"We can't stay here until two o'clock. Let's move toward the center of the map," he decided.

"Got it," she replied.

"But before that, I want to see your map."

He approached her and took out his Satellite Scan terminal, holding it near hers so their maps were synced.

"That gives me more information. Thanks."

Now the screen in his hands featured a map of the route that Anna had run to escape.

She had followed a zigzagging path of over a mile southwest from her starting point in the upper right corner of the map, at which point she turned to the south. From there, she went straight south for two thirds of a mile.

This straight line clearly represented the main road outside. It ran north to south, and if followed, it would eventually lead to a different zone, whatever that turned out to be.

"I want to get past this street as quickly as possible."

"Meaning…in a vehicle of some kind?"

"Yes. Let's do a quick search to see if anything is nearby."

Anna checked her wristwatch: It was 1:35 now. In another five minutes, the scan would start and reveal their location.

"What if we wait here, and then I act as a decoy five minutes from now, and you shoot whatever enemy shows up?" she suggested.

But M was quickly descending the stairs. She followed after him.

"We'll walk and talk. I thought about a leader-decoy strategy, but I got a bad feeling about some bad opponents, so I'd rather not."

"What do you mean?"

"Did you watch the replay video of SJ4? When we were trying to cross the river and swampland at the start of the game."

"I did."

"The self-destructing team called DOOM really busted our ass on the bridge. They're bad news to deal with. They're not trying to win; they just want to perform suicide attacks on famous teams and players. It's not a good idea to antagonize them."

"But that name wasn't on the list of participating teams. We all confirmed it before the match started."

"Right. Which is why I relaxed and let my guard down. That was a mistake. I heard a distant explosion earlier, around 1:28. It was a sound just like distant thunder, when you hear a fireworks show from the next town over. But now I think that was probably a DOOM self-destruct explosion. Their name wasn't on the entry list because they must have figured out that people would know their strategy by now, and they used a different name. There's no rule against it."

"I see…"

M and Anna descended to the first floor and then the exit of the building.

They kept their eyes and ears open for anything out of the ordinary. Once they felt it was safe, they exited onto the street, one at a time.

Once they had walked past the bodies of the two men M shot, they started running south.

"Let's go."

"Roger that!"

Instead of the center of the street, however, they took the left edge.

That gave them a better chance of darting into a building if they started getting shot at. M didn't forget to check upward for open windows as they ran.

Anna followed his example, keeping a distance of at least twenty feet at all times. That was so a single burst of automatic gunfire or a hand grenade couldn't take out both of them at once.

She was the rear guard of their two-person team, so she kept her gun pointed in every direction she looked, including frequent checks behind her. The scariest thing was that someone could wait for them to pass, then sneak up from the rear to ambush them.

Anna was faster than M, so she didn't have to worry about him leaving her behind.

At some intersections, M used a mirror to check around the side. Once they knew it was safe, they would cross the space one at a time.

At 1:36, Anna murmured, "May I ask something?"

"Yeah."

"The suicide-bombing team has five members left at maximum, right?"

"That's right. And make no mistake, their *only* goal is to cause an upset, so they'll head right for the championship contenders. That means one of their targets is SHINC—and that's you."

"Ugh."

She scowled behind her sunglasses. It felt like dealing with stalkers.

"It feels like dealing with stalkers," she admitted aloud. It was probably showing on her face, though she couldn't see it for herself.

"That would be a disaster," M opined.

Really? Coming from you? was a cutdown that Llenn, Fuka-ziroh, or Pitohui would say if they were here.

"But—!"

M suddenly stopped before a particular building, swinging the thick M14 EBR stock at the glass window there. The sturdy glass shattered into pieces that soon vanished.

"We can get away with this."

Beyond the glass was a vehicle waiting to be used.

In our real world, there is a car called the Volkswagen Type 1.

Most people would know it instead as a Beetle, or the VW Bug, and immediately envision the distinct, lovably rounded form of one of the world's most recognizable automobiles: a German classic.

It was created quite a long time ago, in 1938, then produced from 1941 to 2003. A phenomenal number of them were made and sold.

There were modified versions of the Type 1 Beetle for off-road races. Because it was such a simple, plentiful, and cheap vehicle, the Beetle was ideal as a base body for racing modifications.

GGO's version used the Beetle body, then fitted a sturdy pipe roll cage inside the seating area and under the frame for safety. It was tightly constructed, almost like a birdcage.

All extra body parts were also cut off to make it simpler. The lights were shifted from the protruding bumper up to the body, too.

Especially important for off-road duty was the suspension rigging, which was switched to a very sturdy arm system. The shock absorbers and springs were upgraded to a robust racing style. The tires were large and tough for off-roading.

These modifications all made the body considerably wider than the typical Beetle's. Now it looked much more powerful, with longer "legs" that gripped the ground harder.

Tough metal pipe armor extended from the front and back of the vehicle, and sometimes special night-use high beams were attached.

The Beetle's air-cooled flat-four engine was a rear-wheel drive, and this version of the engine was significantly beefed up.

The off-road buggy based on the Beetle chassis was so famously associated with races held in Mexico's Baja California peninsula that the model was popularly known as a Baja Bug, based on both the phrase "Baja buggy" and the base VW Bug.

But M didn't deliver a single word of that explanation. Standing before the bright-yellow Baja Bug on display on the building's ground floor, he simply said to Anna, "I can tell this one will work. Keep an eye out for me."

He waved his left hand to open a menu and started dematerializing his equipment.

The large backpack with the armor plating and the M14 EBR he kept slung over his shoulder vanished in puffs of light. Even the HK45 pistol he kept in a holster on his right thigh vanished.

Now he was unarmed. If an enemy attacked, he could only slap them, punch them, or give them a scissor-poke to the eyes.

He took off his wide-brimmed bush hat and jammed it inside his vest before opening the door to the Baja Bug and sliding carefully into the driver's seat on the left side of the car. There was no window glass on the door.

It wasn't a large vehicle to begin with, and the car had a safety roll cage on the inside. Plus, M was imposingly huge.

From a distance, it seemed impossible that he could fit inside, but this was a game, after all. It would accommodate you, up to a point.

Somehow he managed to get into the seat—and with the ability to reach the shifter as well. M pressed the buttons on the ragged old dashboard full of broken meters rather haphazardly. There were no keys conveniently left around for it.

Suddenly, the Baja Bug, which seemed like nothing more than an abandoned piece of set design, began to protest this assumption. *Is that what you thought about me? Huh?*

Skree-skrun-grun... The starter turned over, and the air-cooled flat-four engine started emitting dry puttering noises in the back.

It belched heavy black smoke that did not suggest the engine was in good shape, but M didn't care. It just needed to run.

"Okay, get in," he ordered.

Anna asked, "What about my gun?"

"Into storage," he said simply.

"......"

Anna was aghast at the idea of going through the next stretch without any weapons but wasn't really in any position to complain about it.

The time was just after 1:38.

In less than two minutes, the scan would start up, and many opponents would make their way toward her, the representative of SHINC on the map. Perhaps one of the suicide bombers would be coming, too.

With a wave of her arm, she put away her Dragunov and Strizh, then tried to get into the passenger seat.

"It's too cramped!"

The pipes above and below made for a miserable experience.

What's the deal with this horribly cramped car? Did they actually design this for people to sit inside?

Moe's most common real-life experience with cars was her father's Lexus LX SUV, with its luxury leather seats, spacious interior, and all-around comfort. She wished she could give this car a taste of the Lexus's medicine. How did that work? Did you put the medicine in the gas tank?

When she got back to reality, she would have to thank her daddy for providing her with the ideal car to ride in. She just had to be careful not to say, "There's plenty of room for a Dragunov rifle in here, Daddy!"

"Ouch!" She bumped her knee on the pipe frame and somehow managed to get herself into the hard, uncomfortable seat.

It was a small car to begin with, and when you added M's size and her own not-insignificant height, their arms were basically in constant contact just from sitting there.

Maybe that would be a moodmaking detail if they were a couple on a romantic date, but this was definitively not that situation. Not in the slightest.

"Your seat belt's a harness. Pull it over your shoulder and waist, then stick the metal buckle in around your midsection. Twist the lever when you need to release it," said M, who was already strapped in.

Anna had an epiphany.

He wasn't warning her because not wearing a seat belt was going to get them written up with a traffic ticket.

"Got it…"

It was because he was going to drive in such a way that a seat belt was an absolute necessity.

Anna did as he said and strapped the thick hanging belts—two over her shoulders and two around her sides—into the round metal buckle. In real life, she would need to tighten the straps according to her size, but because *GGO* was a game, it could manage all of that automatically.

In the good sense, it felt like her body was one with the seat. In the bad sense, the belts were like restraints. She had no escape.

"Okay."

Satisfied that she was strapped in, M pressed down on the accelerator.

Braam, brararararararam! The engine roared to life. He was revving it.

M was not doing this just to hear a lot of noise and annoy the neighbors. By jamming on the gas pedal, he was checking to see if the engine could still accelerate properly.

If you started moving the car without checking, you might promptly stall out in the middle of the road and make a fool of yourself.

M's reflection was in Anna's sunglasses. "Um...just please... drive safely..."

He stomped on the clutch with his left foot and yanked the stick into gear with his right hand.

"Sorry. Just gonna apologize ahead of time."

"Eeeek!"

He pounded the acceleration pedal and violently removed his foot from the clutch.

Gaga-shunk.

The Baja Bug leaped out into the street, shattering the remaining pieces of glass and frame in the ground-level window of the building. Then he yanked left on the wheel.

The Bug's longer suspension sank deep, and everything in the car leaned to the right.

"Hyaaaaaaa!"

Anna screamed again, terrified that the car was going to flip itself over.

Instead, the Baja Bug made a ninety-degree left turn and began to race south down the street.

M put the gear in second, despite the fact that he couldn't see a thing through the fog. Once he got the car good and speeding, he shifted it up again. His use of the stick shift and pedals was ruthless, rapidly bringing the car to a roaring pace.

Once it was in fourth, he let the gas level off. They were already going fifty miles per hour at this point—at least, going by feel, since there was no working speedometer.

Their visibility was about a hundred feet at best, due to the mist. If there was anything in their way up ahead, they would never stop in time, traveling at this speed.

"Um, i-is this s-safe?! If there's anything ahead of us, we'll run into it!" Anna stammered nervously.

"We'll probably be all right," M said casually.

"How can you say that?!"

"There wasn't anything in the street earlier, was there?"

"Oh! Good point…"

Anna had been running down the street to safety and continued on after M rescued her, and she hadn't seen any obstacles like abandoned vehicles in the way. Or building rubble, either.

The street had been very spacious the whole way, with no impediments and no cover that might actually block a bullet, which was why she had to run down it the entire way.

M explained, "If they're going to put thick fog down, it would simply be too sadistic to have a lot of blockage on the roads that might kill you if you run into it. I'm guessing the game designer cut us some slack and cleared out the roads for that reason."

Though Anna didn't know this, M had figured it out earlier when looking down at the street. It was when he had murmured "Interesting" to himself.

"……"

Let's hope that's the case. In fact, please let it be so, Anna thought.

There was nothing but mist straight ahead, so M used the visible buildings on the driver's side of the road to judge the straightness of his driving.

Since the road itself was flat, there wasn't really that much shaking. Thanks to the blessing of the off-road-tuned shock absorbers, which gently removed much of the movement, the sensation of the ride was very strange, like the car itself was floating high over the ground.

"Okay, it's nearly time. Watch the scan for me and point out where on the map we're going."

"G-got it!"

One forty had nearly arrived.

Thanks to her seat belt harness, Anna had trouble reaching her Satellite Scanner, but she eventually managed to work it out of the chest pocket of her vest. She turned it on to see that the scan was starting up.

The dot that said SHINC when touched was her location. The dot was moving, of course, making very fast progress south.

Nearby enemies would be aware of that, too, but unless they had cars of their own, they couldn't catch up.

She reported in with the details. "We're in the upper right quadrant of the map, a bit below the center and moving south! We should pass over the median line in another mile or so!"

"Good report. Is Llenn all right?"

"In the lower left!"

"Good enough. You can put that away now; I wouldn't want you to drop it. Now comes the real test," M warned.

And just to prove his point, someone showed up right then and there.

Not some*one*, but…some car?

The Baja Bug was just racing through a large intersection with another road about as big as the one they were on—when another vehicle roared toward them from the right.

Being in the passenger seat, Anna had a good view of it. "Car to the right!" she called out.

M glanced over briefly. The other car was a silver coupe with four round headlights and an emblem of a running horse in the center of the grill.

They must have known the Bug was coming; the car was already making a right turn to intersect with their path.

Fortunately, they didn't have enough of a lead to collide. The coupe made a turn in the intersection, rear wheels sliding wildly. The pursuit of the Baja Bug had begun.

It took M only that single glance to identify the other car. "That's a first-model Ford Mustang. A historical automobile. Haven't seen one of those in *GGO* before. Is it a Squad Jam exclusive? I wanna ride in it," he said happily.

"Is that all you care about?! It could be one of those self-destruct sickos in there!" Anna cried, watching the silver car behind them in the rearview mirror.

For about two and a half seconds, the two cars were simply

going for a drive. The Mustang was following the Baja Bug at a distance of about seventy-five feet.

"No, it's not them."

"How can you tell?"

"Because he would have blown himself up already. This distance is close enough. We'd be dead."

"……"

That's a good point, Anna thought.

And right at that moment—*crunch!*

The Mustang's driver sped up rapidly and hit them with the priceless vehicle. Although faded and dusty, the body had been pristine—until now. There was a big dent in the front, and one of the headlights was broken.

It was a ruthless attack that jolted the Baja Bug violently. M carefully adjusted the steering wheel and kept their course straight.

"Yep, they're faster than us. No wonder, with that sports coupe."

"Now's not the time for being impressed!"

"But they're not good at collisions. You can't stop a car by ramming into it. If you want to stop the car in front, you've got to push on one of the two rear tires. That'll make them go sideways or spin out. The police use that technique all the time in America. It works in *GGO*, too, so remember that one for later."

"Now's not the time for giving educational speeches!"

Anna did not want to ride in the car anymore while M was driving.

Prattattattattatta!

Some lightweight gunfire erupted behind them.

Clank, cla-cla-clank.

The bullets bounced dryly off the body of the Bug.

"We're getting shot!"

"Right. You get shot?"

"No!"

This, frankly, was a confusing sequence of statements. Let's translate them into a more helpful vocabulary.

"I can confirm by observation that this car is being shot at by a gun, M."

"That is true, Anna. By the way, I am just fine. Did you happen to be struck by any of those bullets? I'm very worried about your safety."

"Your kind concern is most appreciated. Fortunately, I am not aware of any such damage."

With busted-up side mirrors that were somehow still attached, Anna and M took a look at the Mustang trailing them by seventy feet.

There was someone sitting in the driver's seat, of course, but there was also a passenger leaning forward with a gun. It was an MP5A4, an H&K SMG.

Whomever it was, they fired again.

M pulled the wheel a little bit to avoid the bullets. They didn't make any sound on the Bug.

"There are two of them. Not any of our friends obviously."

"Wh-what should we do?"

"We're in trouble if they pull up alongside us. Maybe we can lose them."

He turned the wheel slightly, bringing the Baja Bug over to the left side of the street. The wheels were almost coming into contact with the raised sidewalk.

This was to prevent the Mustang from getting on their left side. The passenger seat was on the right side, so this meant the armed man there couldn't shoot directly at them.

Then M put the car back down a gear and floored the gas. The Baja Bug's body tilted backward as it bolted forward. The engine in the rear was practically screaming with the revolutions per minute it was doing now. This was just before the red zone, where you weren't supposed to put any more stress on it. Or maybe it was already there.

"Aieeee!"

Anna's face was locked in a grimace. She clutched the seat belt, not that it was going to make any difference if they got hit.

M took them as far as he could in third gear before putting the car in fourth, the top gear. At this point, he was bottoming out the pedal; it couldn't go any farther. The Baja Bug's speed felt like it was topping out at about sixty miles per hour.

That was its highest speed as an item, it seemed.

And it was not a speed to be driving at in heavy fog. Even without the visibility issue, that was not a city driving speed.

But that was not enough.

"They're still back there."

The Mustang was hanging around at a distance behind them. It was probably holding back some power, since that type of muscle car could do better. It was staying behind them, figuring the route was safe if the lead car didn't hit any obstacles.

Anna was disappointed. Sooo disappointed.

They'd decided that there wouldn't be any obstacles in the road, but did neither M nor the Mustang driver consider the possibility that they might come up on a T-intersection and run straight into a building?

"Ah!"

The next moment, she saw something.

Through the windshield, a person emerged from the mist.

It was just for a brief moment, but the person was neither a teammate nor one of the familiar other members of LPFM. It didn't seem to be a person from any of the heavy favorites.

And the instant she saw them, they were already out of sight.

Boom. The player was thrown over the top of the car by the Baja Bug's pipe-frame bumper, where he promptly vanished.

"Huh? O-oh…was that…?" she stammered.

"Yeah, I ran someone over," he replied. "But I saw them in that split second. Don't worry—it wasn't a friend. And even if it was, Llenn would have jumped over us, I bet."

"……"

Whichever team and whomever it was, they were really unlucky.

It's just a game; forgive us, Anna prayed to their memory.

M glanced at the side mirror and saw the Mustang was keeping pace. "They're still hanging on. I was hoping the guy I just ran over would have hit them on the way down," he said casually. It was only a game.

The two in the Mustang seemed to have decided that shooting or hitting them was needlessly risky and had switched to a more reliable plan. They were going to keep following, persistently ensuring that the other car didn't get away. And that kind of foe was a much more annoying problem to deal with than someone who would keep attacking.

After another ten seconds of parallel racing, M said, "We're nearly at the median line between north and south." Though this was based on nothing but a physical hunch, since nothing on the dashboard worked. "I wonder what's beyond that point. Let's just pray it's terrain we can cross safely."

Apparently, he intended to keep racing through without slowing down.

Anna blanched. "Wh-what if it's a wasteland?"

"That's not bad. We'll be fine as long as we don't run into the rocks dotting the landscape. We'll just keep riding and staying away until we run out of fuel. And if it's a residential area, there will be streets. If it's a river, we'll jump in and then swim. The worst would be forest, I suppose. If we slam into a big tree, we're dead," he said, strangely pleased with the options.

Anna *definitely* did not want to ride in the car anymore while M was driving.

Onward through the valley of buildings, the Baja Bug fled and the Mustang pursued.

On the left-hand sidewalk stood a player.

"Oof..."

Despite the screaming of the engine, Anna heard M grunt. It was a pained, bitter sound the likes of which she'd never heard him make.

"What is it?" she asked.

"Brace for impact. Hopefully, we'll both survive. Good luck," he replied.

"Huh? Oh..."

Understanding sank in as the sounds escaped her mouth.

She had only seen a blur and no real physical details of the player. But M had.

And he saw that it was a member of DOOM.

When he saw two cars loudly racing down the street next to him, the man gleefully shouted, "One of them's gotta be SHINC!"

He grabbed one of the many strings placed all over his body and pulled it.

"I'll blow 'em both up!"

He exploded.

The second major blast of SJ5 was about the same power as the first.

The only difference was that this one happened between tall buildings.

Inevitably, the shock it produced struck the structures on either side, but while they deteriorated a little, the sturdy metal-reinforced concrete buildings resisted total collapse.

Meaning that they reflected the force of the explosion.

The force of the shock bouncing off one building proceeded to reflect off another building. As these reflections added up, they naturally made their way toward more open spaces.

In other words, over the street running between all those buildings.

Anna saw the reflection in the Baja Bug's side mirror turn orange for an instant.

It was an almost romantic moment, like the sun crossing the mirror while on a sunset drive.

But in reality, it was the polar opposite of that: a moment of pure, ominous destruction.

The orange light disappeared, and the impact hit a second later.

The shock wave of the explosion caught up to the car traveling sixty miles per hour and blew past it as easily as taking candy from a baby.

While the street was very wide, it was still narrow for an empty space, and the shock wave that ripped through it was amplified by bouncing off the buildings, to an extent that only the computer system running *GGO* could determine.

At any rate, it was an incredibly powerful shock wave that first hit the Mustang, which was in the rear position.

The back of the car lifted easily off the ground, which only caused the boxy body to receive *more* pressure from the explosion, instantly flipping it into the air. The Mustang spun and spun, vertically and horizontally, like a dead leaf whipped up by a sudden gust of wind.

"Hyaaa!" screamed the man gripping the skinny steering wheel.

"Bwauh!" added the passenger with the MP5A4. Compelled by the power of centrifugal force, they were pulled right out of the car through the open windows.

This was at a height of about a hundred feet. The two men, much lighter than the car, were that much easier to toss around by the explosive force.

The driver slammed into the side of the building on the left side of the street, which killed him instantly.

The other one flew through a cloud of broken glass shards, one large piece completely bisecting his body. He, too, was done with SJ5.

The priceless Mustang floating through the air like a scattered piece of aluminum foil landed roof-first on one of the building's supports, warping and wrapping itself around it, a total husk of a vehicle.

M probably would have lamented the loss of such a classic car if he had the time to actually react to it.

Boom!

The powerful sound enveloped the Baja Bug, and then M and Anna felt themselves flying.

The shock wave kicked the Bug into the air like an empty aluminum can. It was as though the car had suddenly turned into a rocket and shot at a diagonal.

With some vertical rotation as well, the rounded, small body spun and followed a parabola. And on the inside...

"Urgh!" M groaned.

"Aaaaaaaaaahhhh!" Anna shrieked, very ladylike.

There was nothing they could do now. They were trapped in the car.

"Stay calm, Anna. We're both strapped in. We might still survive the fall back down."

"Aaaaaaaaah!"

There was a gale-force roar outside, but because of the comm, they could each clearly hear the other.

"If you freak out too much, the AmuSphere will auto–shut down because of it."

"Hyaaaaaaa!

"....."

A few seconds before the Baja Bug finally touched the ground once more, M murmured, "Elza Kanzaki's next song is a tearjerker ballad."

"What? Really? I can't wait!"

"Now, prepare for impact."

Boom!

The rotating Baja Bug landed—by sheer coincidence—facing the same direction it had been driving already, tires down.

But it was not the kind of cool, safe landing you saw in action movies.

Ba-gur-chank!

The shocks absorbed impact as they deployed, but naturally, they could not neutralize all of the force of the fall, and they blew right off the attachments.

All four tires immediately exploded, and the inner wheels themselves each shot outward like spring-loaded toys.

Having lost its legs in the moment of impact, the car's chassis hit the ground at last, slightly softer than before but still with furious force.

"Hgah!"

"Eeeek!"

M and Anna were hit with fierce vertical pressure as well as a damage assessment. Both of them immediately lost two-fifths of their health, perhaps because the game decided they had broken their spines.

But if they hadn't had the amount of impact absorbed by the tires and suspension blowing up or if they'd landed roof-first, they both would have died instantly.

And after hitting the ground—the car bounced.

With nothing left but the body, the Bug flipped headfirst, bounding to a height of fifteen feet, still soaring. At the peak of its arc, it lost balance and turned sideways, started falling, and landed again.

This time it tumbled spectacularly, flipping and turning as its forward momentum continued—beneath a reddened sky and over tight, packed snow.

By the time it had already done seventeen sideways rotations and failed to complete the last one, rolling back flat on the ground with a thud, the Baja Bug was no longer recognizable as a car.

It was merely a pipe-metal cage with a few metal panels that suggested the appearance of a car.

There were no doors left, no roof, and it might as well never have had an engine to start with. All these parts were now littered across the snowfield along the route the Bug had taken.

The top and bottom of the cage had reversed from what they were when it was riding on its tires.

But firmly located on the inside were two seats, along with seat belts that held their human occupants in place.

M could feel virtual blood rising into his virtual head. "Anna... you still alive?" he asked. There had been so much whiplash that his neck hurt too much to turn it.

"No, I'm already dead," she replied firmly. "I've died at least three times, and that's just what I remember. I am now a ghost. You can believe that because I'm the one telling you."

"Owww...," M grumbled, and craned his neck to the right, feeling about a hundred times worse than when he simply woke up on the wrong side of the bed. He saw the profile of a pretty blond girl there with her mouth hanging open. It was impossible to tell if she was alive or dead just from looking at her.

Her cap had flown off, and her hair hung in wild, loose strands.

But the sunglasses were perfectly on point.

"Don't take your seat belt off yet. Watch how I do it," M said. He was going to demonstrate how to properly escape the upturned vehicle—although the Baja Bug no longer qualified as a vehicle.

First he reached for the roof—which was now just the pipe cage—below his head with his dominant right hand and pushed. He also applied pressure with both feet.

Only then could he use his left hand to undo the buckle.

The instant he was loose, all of his weight was going to push downward, mostly on his right arm, so he held firm with his limbs and quickly added his left hand for support to keep himself from falling.

If you undid the seat belt without any preparation, you'd fall right on your head and possibly even break your neck. That was the one thing that had to be avoided at all costs.

Then M crawled out of the birdcage and tumbled onto the hard white snow. He got to his feet, fighting back dizziness, and circled around to Anna's seat.

"Pardon my reach."

He held up her upside-down body to help her get out of the seat. She, too, managed to crawl out of the car on her own.

Once out of the pipe-metal birdcage, they both leaned against it. Each one went into the menu to use an emergency med kit. The hit points slowly began to return to their avatars.

Only then did they finally survey the spectacle around them.

"Ooh…this is amazing…"

"It's kind of beautiful… Both the sky and the town…"

M and Anna beheld the reddish-blue of the sky.

The air pressure of the explosion had blown clear all of the fog in the surrounding area, including the sky. Beneath that clearing, the ruined city area on the northeast of the map, where they had just been, was clearly, crisply visible.

They were standing witness to a sight that you would never, ever see in real life.

Half of the massive buildings had crumbled and fallen. It was literally a mountain of rubble. Around them, other buildings were still in the process of toppling, lifting huge dust clouds into the air. They could feel the rumbling of the collapse through their feet.

The explosion had destroyed dozens of buildings nearest to it and altered the landscape. The main road was now completely sealed off and inaccessible. They'd have to redraw the maps.

A massive mushroom cloud was rising over the city. It was like an actual giant mushroom, growing with the nutrients it had taken from dozens of buildings.

The field of snow they now stood in started as abruptly as if someone had drawn a line marking the end of the city. It was a brilliantly vivid boundary line and looked like someone had just pasted the map data there and called it a day. Maybe the person making the map had gotten bored of it.

The boundary, presumably, was the north-south median line.

They were now about five hundred yards south of that boundary line. They'd been hurled most of that distance by the blast and tumbled the rest of the way.

The fog had been too thick to see the actual explosion when it happened, and it'd been even less possible to be aware of what was going on once they'd been picked up by the blast, but it would seem that they had just barely gotten out of the city when it happened.

The fog was clear around the snowfield, too, and everything was totally flat.

M turned around to see. The horizon was not visible, of course, but they could see white for several hundred yards in each direction.

"Ugh!" he grunted.

He'd noticed a number of little sesame-seed dots. Not just on the snowfield but also at the base of the city and around the boundary line: little moving dots.

"Unfortunately, we don't have the luxury of time to relax."

"Huh?"

The wind picked up.

A strong gale rushed out from the base of the mushroom cloud, picking up distant mist. The snowfield, the rubble, the massive buildings—they were quickly becoming occluded again.

"I saw one or two dozen people in the area. All the players who were staying put in the snowfield saw us and are on their way."

"Whaaat?!"

Anna was finally coming to recognize the significant danger of their situation.

M swung his left arm to call up his menu so he could go through his inventory. Anna started the process as well.

They brought their gear back out. Motes of light appeared, taking the shape of guns and protective wear.

"Wh-what do we do?" asked Anna, who had only around half her health left.

"If we want to survive, we have to fight," replied M, who had a bit over 60 percent.

"Can we run?"

"They were coming from the city side, too. We're already surrounded."

"Oh no… I think this is the end of my decoy stint as team leader, Boss…"

"Too early to give up."

M lowered his newly manifested backpack off his shoulders. He opened it and turned it upside down, dumping out the contents.

It was the armor plating (or shield) that had played such a huge role in Squad Jams past, saving his life and the lives of his teammates on so many occasions.

He quickly undid the joints that held them together and explained, "We'll make use of this dead car for a bit longer. I can attach these to the frame and set up a defensive outpost for us."

"Oh…"

He pulled the plates into their individual pieces. Each one was twenty inches long and twelve inches wide. There were eight of them, so they could cover quite a lot of area in total.

But if their opponents were firing wildly at full auto, bullets would most certainly find their way through the cracks.

"Fortunately, we're both snipers who can fire semi-auto. We'll stay here and shoot back at anyone who comes for us as soon as we see them. Prepare yourself for combat."

"……"

"Or would you prefer to surrender and leave your teammates behind?"

She didn't answer him with words.

Instead, she picked up her Dragunov, pulled the loading lever, and sent the first bullet into the chamber.

CHAPTER 9
Converging, Part 2

SECT.9

CHAPTER 9
Converging, Part 2

At one forty-five, Shirley heard the sounds of fierce combat while she was skiing across the snowfield alone.

The sounds were coming from the right, in the direction she was currently traveling. She'd been skiing all over the snow the whole time, so her map of the area was pretty considerable at this point.

Thanks to that, she knew the area thoroughly, as well as her current facing. Her skis were pointed north-northwest, which meant the gunfire was coming from...

"The north. What now...?" she wondered.

The gunfire was happening ceaselessly from a distance of several hundred yards, perhaps a thousand. Although it wasn't clear, there was too much happening for it to be just one or two people.

"That explosion led to some activity..."

She had confirmed the explosion of one of the members of DOOM earlier—who had registered under the team tag BOKR this time. That had been at 1:41.

The sky looking so clear and bright to the north for most of a minute must have been caused by the explosion sweeping away all the fog. It was back again now.

That must have revealed the locations of several players to one another. It was the first sound of true, fierce combat she'd heard that day. There had to be at least ten people involved.

"In that case…"

If there were that many people absorbed in their fight at the moment, she could sneak up behind them and snipe to her heart's content.

"Guess I'll go and poke them in the back."

Shirley headed off with her skis.

One minute later, Shirley was somewhat disappointed.

"What's with them? Are they just target practice mannequins?"

It was all too easy to pick off her targets.

She'd made steady progress through the mist, until she could hear the gunshots and see the muzzle flares at the same time. Her targets were facing and shooting in the other direction, so they had no idea she was there.

As time passed, the fog had gotten thinner, so now she could see about a hundred feet. Shirley stopped at that distance and scanned the area. She lazily steadied her R93 Tactical 2 and pulled the trigger.

A man on his stomach firing his gun took an exploding bullet to the neck and died. He had no idea how it had happened.

"I'm telling you, you've gotta watch your six," Shirley lectured her second victim as she shot him thirty seconds later.

He, too, was shooting at something he could see through the mist. But while it was visible to him, it was not to Shirley, except for the fact that it was a dark blob in the distance, considerably larger than a human.

There were also occasional muzzle flashes from it, so someone there was shooting back.

"A car…?"

She tried looking through the scope, but that didn't help much. And she wasn't going to shoot what she couldn't identify.

But if it was a car, she was curious as to why it wasn't running. It must have been driven out to this location.

Did the tires get shot out? Maybe it ran out of fuel.

"This is starting to get boring…"

A minute later, she was taking out two more players.

She was making a very wide circle around the mysterious black object when she spotted two men whose clothes were different styles, which meant they probably weren't squadmates.

They were about ten feet apart, one shooting a machine gun from the ground while the other moved forward.

Bam, ch-chik, bam.

Shirley shot one, loaded up, and shot the other.

The world was quiet again. They were probably the last two survivors. With the gunfight over and silence back, Shirley got down on the ground, curious about the black object.

If someone was over there, she wanted to help kill them.

She couldn't get close enough to see because there was no cover in the snowfield. If she tried crawling along the ground and they saw even a glimpse of her, she'd get mercilessly shot to pieces.

"Oh! There is a way," she realized aloud.

There *was* an object that would protect her from bullets, and it was on the ground just sixty feet away from her. Two of them, in fact.

Shirley put her skis and poles into her inventory for the moment, replacing them with crampons for her shoes. Those were the spiked cleats that mountain climbers typically wore to keep their feet from slipping.

She crawled on hands and feet up to the man's dead body at an angle that kept her hidden behind it, stopping just before the DEAD tag floating overhead. The shape of the car was much clearer from here.

She rested the barrel of the R93 Tactical 2 rifle atop the body and thought, *Here we go…*

Now it was just a battle of stamina.

Digging her crampons into the snow behind her, she started engaging in a sheer show of strength: pushing the dead body forward from a prone position.

The body was an indestructible object now and could not be broken down further, but it wasn't totally immobile. Otherwise a player stuck under a dead body would be completely helpless and trapped for the next ten minutes until the corpse finally vanished.

The friction coefficient of the smooth, packed snow was low, and with each kick against the ground with her crampons, Shirley slid the body forward a good amount. She was exhibiting a powerful bowlegged style here.

As she got closer, she could see more and more about the car.

First of all, it was not a car.

It was a mysterious thing that she had never seen or heard of before in *GGO*: an object consisting of a pipe frame with protective armor plates attached.

And when she looked through the scope, she saw M and Anna inside it.

"Oh, it's you guys. No need to shoot you, then."

Both of them were glowing with damage effects all over, making them an oddly beautiful sight in the hazy fog. They looked like gaming PCs with red LEDs inside the case.

"I'm amazed you're still alive, looking like that," Shirley muttered.

✳   ✳   ✳

"I was certain that I was dead this time."

"Same…"

"I owe you my thanks, Shirley."

"Same…"

"Fine, fine. Just keep walking, you two. Or you really will die."

Shirley was in the lead on her skis, with Anna and M forming a line behind her as they trudged south over the snow and through the fog.

It was 1:53.

*   *   *

About four minutes earlier, having confirmed that there were no other enemies around, Shirley shouted over to M, alerting him that one of his allies was there. He responded by summoning her.

Shirley got to her feet and walked over, where she saw giant M and not-tiny Anna squashed inside a metal-frame cage. M's shield plates were strung up around them, attached with duct tape.

"Thanks. I was just sticking them up at random, and after getting shot so much, I'm too numb to get out," M said pathetically.

From there, Shirley could see a whole array of DEAD tags scattered around the place. Most of them were to the north, maybe ten or so. They were the people M had sniped. He sure had killed a lot of people.

Anna had done her share of the heavy lifting, too, as there were more bodies in the other directions Shirley hadn't come from.

So they had taken a position here, put up shields to protect themselves, and persevered despite the many shots that snuck through the gaps between the shield pieces.

It was frankly miraculous that they had survived after taking so many hits, though. It must have been because all the hits were to their extremities and not in fatal locations.

Shirley used her ken-nata knife to chop up all the duct tape, until M and Anna could finally escape their cage.

Now she could see M's hit point bar for herself. The bar was very short, maybe at 10 percent, though it was currently growing after he'd used his emergency med kit.

"I'm alive...," Anna murmured, clutching her sniper rifle. Her number was probably around the same.

Inside and around the cage, in fact, was a veritable pile of empty ten-shot magazines for Anna's Dragunov and twenty-shot magazines for M's M14 EBR.

How much shooting must they have done? Presumably, quite a lot of covering fire to keep enemies away. The majority of the gunfire Shirley had heard from a distance must have been M and Anna.

Had they used up just about all the ammo they had? If not for the recharge, they would have almost entirely expended all their battle ability.

"Nearly time for the scan. Want to watch it here?" Shirley asked.

M was putting the shield back in his pack. "Yes," he said at once. "But we'll need to move again as soon as we watch it."

"Why is that?"

"Because Anna's the team leader for SHINC. Enemies will come swarming us. The self-destructing team is here under a different name, and there are still four of them left. It was one of them earlier who blasted our car all the way out of the city."

"I see..."

And after watching the scan results at 1:50, they proceeded to travel south.

"You sure you don't want to hook up to the comm with us?" asked M from the rear as they trudged through the snow. When he had mentioned this first, she casually declined.

"I can hear you fine right now. Plus, I'm still going after Pitohui. This scattered starting point rule in SJ5 was practically created for my benefit. So once I've seen you off safely to the south, I'm gonna split."

"I see. Do as you like."

Anna asked, "Why do you say it's safe to the south?"

Quite matter-of-factly, Shirley replied, "Because most of the players who were in the snow from the start I've already eliminated. One of them was one of the self-destructing sickos with a giant backpack. Oh, and don't worry. I didn't see any SHINC folks. They must have fled to a different area."

"I see..."

"Go about two miles south and turn right to the west. If you're lucky, you'll meet up with Llenn."

They continued traveling south from there.

Although the trio was out of sight, there was one player who could overhear them.

*   *   *

At 1:50, three players watched the scan roll in while squished in a very cramped, undersized basement: Llenn, Fukaziroh, and Boss.

From what they learned, there were twenty-five teams remaining. The fighting was picking up around the map, and five teams had lost all six members by this point.

"When they didn't even get the chance to regroup... Poor things..."

"Oh, Llenn. Your compassion for your enemies is your worst habit. Let us be honest and celebrate instead."

"Yeah, I guess so."

Naturally, MMTM, ZEMAL, and SHINC were still among the living.

MMTM's dot had moved from the upper left corner closer to the middle but was still firmly within that quadrant.

Most likely it meant that he didn't have to worry about a hiding spot. Whoever had taken over the leader slot from David was not pushing their luck.

ZEMAL was in the lower right corner. Right on the corner. Almost no movement there.

"Oh, I know what's going on here," noted Fukaziroh. "Since he's at the edge of the map, the enemy can only come from ahead of him. So he can keep shooting without worrying about his back."

"Ah, I see... And whatever dark shapes he sees ahead of him, he can shoot without fear," Llenn echoed.

With their machine-gun firepower and the ammo refills, that

was a valid strategy to win fights this time around. Apparently, there wasn't a member of DOOM who had gone after him yet.

SHINC's dot, meaning Anna, had gone quite far south, out of the upper right quadrant and over into the lower right.

"She's moved a whole bunch. Anna's been putting in the work." Boss grinned.

As a matter of fact, she *had* been working harder than anyone else, but she'd also nearly died several times over.

The scan was over. There were no team leader dots within two miles of Llenn's current position, at least. But—not to belabor the point—that did not mean there were no enemies around.

"Let's get a move on! To the east!" Llenn said.

Boss asked, "Sure, but why?"

"It's the direction the sun rises. Believe it or not, Llenn was a sunflower in a previous life," Fukaziroh replied.

Llenn ignored her. "To get closer to Anna. Also, I think all those guys we beat mostly came from the east. So the enemy density over there should be lighter."

"That makes sense. But even if we do run into anyone, we can have fun killing them. I'll take the lead in front of you, Llenn."

"But then we won't be able to see!"

"That's not what she means, Fuka."

So the three of them left the cellar.

The fog was supposed to clear entirely in the next ten minutes, but while it did seem lighter than before, the range of vision was still only forty yards at best.

Taking point was Boss, with her silenced Vintorez sniper rifle set to automatic. She was watching the path ahead and also to the right.

Five yards behind her, wrapped in a poncho and carrying a P90 with a muzzle silencer, was Llenn. She was watching the territory ahead and also to the left.

Three yards behind *her* was Fukaziroh, with a grenade launcher in each hand. She was the rear guard, so it was her job to watch behind them.

They could have Llenn and Fukaziroh travel inside the *PM*, with Boss hiding behind it for cover from bullets—but that would slow them down and, more importantly, lower their attack power, so they decided it was best to travel with their favorite weapons instead.

Since it was still misty, they did not run. Instead, they traveled at about a speedwalk, by Boss's standards.

They were making their way through the dead bodies they'd created themselves when Boss murmured, "I'm impressed that you were able to team up with Shinohara earlier. I would have thought they'd hate that."

Without losing her focus on the sights and sounds around them, Llenn chimed in, "Yeah, you were saying something about your 'Shinohara connection.'"

Boss was aware that Fukaziroh's real name was Miyu Shinohara, which was why Llenn didn't feel bad about bringing it up.

"Oh, that's simple. I found Shinohara blasting away with his machine gun at the switchyard, thought he seemed like a good partner to have, and just followed him at a safe distance."

"Even though M said to stay hidden in a safe place until the mist was gone…?"

"I was laying it by fear."

"You mean, playing it by ear?"

"Yeah, that. Anyway, while the machine gun is powerful, he's just one guy. When he was shooting one guy and the other one was circling around behind him, I took it upon myself to blast the second guy with a grenade."

"I see."

"And through the mist, I shouted over to Shinohara that I'd saved him. I even revealed my real name. I said, 'We're probably unrelated relatives!' and for some strange reason, he believed me. He said, 'Well, if we're both Shinoharas, I guess I got no choice.' Honestly, I'd like to know what in the world made him think he had no choice. How does that work?"

"So you're saying…you teamed up with him by claiming you had a close personal connection…while you were conspiring to kill him the entire time…?" Llenn said, aghast.

What can you say? Fukaziroh was, as it turned out, still Fukaziroh.

"It was a sacrificial action, revealing my own name in the belief that sticking with him would give me a chance to take out Vivi… and it *almost* worked out… So how are you gonna make it up to me, Llenn?" she said, glaring at her friend.

"Dunno. Don't care," Llenn replied.

Five minutes later, it was 1:56.

"In the midst of a forest of great, huge trees, Llenn encountered a wild Pitohui."

"I don't need your weird narration, Fuka."

The residential area ended as suddenly and unnaturally as though it was split by a ruler, at which point the next area began: a forest of huge, thick trees. Within, they met a suspicious-looking woman in a navy bodysuit with face tattoos.

The only reason they didn't get into a shoot-out in the fog was because Pitohui spotted them first and started a dialogue.

Now the four were hunched beside a large tree, keeping an eye on every direction and conversing quietly through their comms.

"I was wondering why there were no enemies along the way… Now it makes sense," said Boss.

Since entering the forest, they had seen dead bodies lying here and there. DEAD tags gleamed all over the place.

Clearly, Pitohui had done in all of them. Every player wandering around the forest was dead now.

Pitohui smirked happily and said, "Hey, guys. Glad to see you're all doing well. What kind of fun stuff did you run into before this? Because I had nothing. I just hid inside a hollow tree and killed every person who wandered past me—that's all."

Llenn replied, "We went through so much, it'd be hard to

describe it all. But mainly, Fukaziroh did something really crazy. We need to have an intervention for her later so she can apologize."

"What?!"

"Listen, I'd be happy to hear the whole story after the game's over. For now, let's focus on the combat."

"May I just ask one question first, Pitohui?" Boss said, picking up on something.

Pitohui replied, "What is it?"

"If you started in the woods area, you must have noticed the team that banded together to go after Llenn's bounty. They were calling out for one another, recruiting members in the mist, I assume. So you were aware of that…and you let them go?"

"Ah!" Llenn gasped, louder than she meant to.

Boss's perception was remarkable, and Llenn was equally shocked at her own lack of the same, but the most obnoxious thing of all was Pitohui's choice of action. It had made things so much harder and for no good reason.

"Hmm? Really? Is that what happened?" said Pitohui, desperately trying and failing to play dumb.

"Honestly, you…"

Oh? Is Boss going to yell at her for me? Is she going to scold Pitohui for being a bad teammate and friend? Yes, Boss! Give her an earful! Llenn thought.

"…are a genius, Pitohui! I must follow your model of behavior! No more coddling my teammates, either!"

Hang on, snapped Llenn in her mind as swiftly as a quick-shooting gunman.

"Very good, Boss. You understand the mentality of a leader."

Wait a second. No, that's not right. Boss is only puffing you up with hot air because she knows you're Elza Kanzaki.

"I'm honored by your compliments. Wah-ha-ha!"

"Oh, it's fully earned, I assure you. Wah-ha-ha!"

Okay, forget these two, Llenn thought. Surely there was a more substantive topic to discuss.

So instead, she asked, "What do we do now?"

Pitohui's laugh immediately died. "Hmm? We'll wait for two o'clock here, then think of what to do," she said matter-of-factly.

"Yeah…I guess that's best."

Llenn changed from her white camo poncho to a green one.

*　　　*　　　*

At 1:58, Shirley was in the midst of the snowfield.

"All right, my guide work ends now. Just keep going west from here."

In real life, Mai worked as a nature guide, but she never expected to be playing a similar role at any point in *GGO*.

Of course, in real life she would never abandon her guide position like this. If she did that in Hokkaido, someone was likely to get eaten by a bear. Nature could test you, it was true, but the point of a guided hike was not to get your customers devoured.

"Thank you. You've been a huge help," said M, whose hit points had recovered to halfway and were still rising because he had used his final med kit.

"I appreciate it," said Anna, who'd recovered to a bit over 30 percent but had already used up all her med kits and couldn't heal any further. Even still, she gave a very courteous and diligent Japanese bow.

"Hey, M," Shirley called out once the two had started walking again.

It was definitely a classic movie thing to wait to say the most important thing until after people started walking away. Shirley was probably aiming for that effect.

"Yeah?" M replied without turning.

She stared at his back with a fierce smile on her lips. "I'm the one who's going to kill Pitohui. Just try to stop me. I've always wanted to fight you, too."

"Got it."

He waved his hand over his shoulder.

But did not turn to look.

"I mean, you could do that now," Anna murmured into the comm.

"It wouldn't be sporting. Besides, Pitohui enjoys it this way."

"Well, if you say so… That's fine."

"This is a game. It's for fun. You don't actually die," M said wistfully.

Of course, Anna remembered that in SJ2, Pitohui and M had risked their actual lives on their avatar's lives in the game.

"Very true!" She beamed. While she looked like an exotic foreign beauty, her response was more befitting of who she really was on the inside: a teenage girl.

"Okay, let's run."

"Got it!"

Shirley watched the two of them vanish into the mist, trading lines like the final scene of some coming-of-age movie.

"I thought they might turn around and shoot me…".

She let go of the R93 Tactical 2 hanging over her chest. If either of them had turned and pointed their gun at her, she would have fired at the giant man first.

"It's too bad. This would have been a great chance to take out M."

What a shame. She'd lost that chance.

Into the comm, Shirley said, "Hey, thanks for waiting. Shall we meet up now?"

*   *   *

It was not actually any participant in SJ5 who was most eagerly awaiting two o'clock, when the fog was supposed to be fully cleared away at last.

"Ten more seconds!"

It was the dozens of players in the big pub, watching on the screens there.

"Nine!"

For the past hour, they'd been almost blind to whatever was happening.

"Eight!"

As soon as SJ5 started, the huge monitors displaying the action of the big game were completely white, all thanks to the obscuring fog.

Occasionally, the players would see the flash of gun muzzles and the resulting glowing DEAD tag, but that was about all they could actually make out.

"Seven!"

Naturally, the audience protested.

The jeers were constant. "What the hell is this?" they shouted. "Give us our money back!" Nobody had actually paid any money for this.

Eventually, the special rules were pointed out, and the audience begrudgingly accepted them as long as it was only until the fog cleared up, and they continued drinking in the meantime. Except the fog didn't clear up. Not at all.

Some of them were so fed up that they simply left and didn't come back.

"Six!"

Even when fiercer battles broke out, the cameras did not zoom in especially close to capture them. Seeing hazy muzzle flashes in a sea of white did not exactly paint a vivid picture of what was happening.

Maybe if the cameras could at least be turned to thermal vision, there might be more definition of the action unfolding—but that was not happening, either.

The cameras had gone on thermal mode in SJ2, when Llenn and Fukaziroh burned pink smoke in the jungle, but not this time. There was no reason given, but it was probably because doing it for all the cameras would have been too much trouble on the system or something.

"Five!"

So the people in the bar counting down the last seconds until the hour was up were the patient ones who'd been sticking around the whole time.

"Four!"

But they also had a lurking concern.

Why had none of the players who died in SJ5 returned to the bar yet?

"Three!"

Yes, no one had come back after being disqualified. And that did not make sense.

In all previous Squad Jams, you had to wait ten minutes after dying before you were returned to the bar. Then you could hang out and watch the rest of the event with the audience or talk about your results with your other teammates or the crowd as it went on.

They could have come back to the bar and simply stayed in a private room with their teammates, but the chances of every single deceased player doing that had to be almost zero.

It wasn't clear whether the mystery was going to be resolved anytime soon, but the clock counted down each second regardless.

"Two!"

It was 1:59:58. Almost time.

"One!"

1:59:59.

"Zero!"

✳   ✳   ✳

The players gathered on the map of SJ5 at that exact moment were greeted with a true spectacle.

Those waiting on their wristwatches or ocular overlay clocks knew that the mist was supposed to clear out at exactly two o'clock.

If they were standing in the midst of a wide-open area, then the moment after the mist cleared, they might be sniped at from a far distance. There had to be one or two snipers thinking of doing exactly that.

So all the players were staying as low as possible, hiding behind cover, when the moment arrived.

And that's when they saw it.

Llenn, Fukaziroh, Pitohui, and Boss were on the ground in the forest.

The moment it turned two o'clock, they saw the white fog instantly and silently vanish.

"Wow!" Llenn exclaimed, unable to stop herself.

It was a beautiful sight.

In a single instant, the forest was restored to a forest again, making visible the distant rows of trees, the greenery of the plants, and the brown soil of the earth.

It was positively magical.

M and Anna experienced the same effect.

This was because they had just reached the end of the snowfield and entered the rather abrupt forest zone. They were prone on the ground with a huge tree in between. Anna looked up in the moment and was entranced by what she saw.

M, however, was staring right at his Satellite Scanner.

"Ahhh…"

Shirley saw it happen as she lay prone in the snow.

The scenery around her suddenly expanded, so in three seconds, she could see as far as one possibly could.

She also saw the green of the forest where she was heading, a few hundred yards to the west.

"Shit!" she snapped. "It's already time!"

*   *   *

"Whoaaa!"

"Here it is!"

"You can see the terrain!"

The audience in the pub erupted into noise.

On the large monitors hung high on the walls, the mist had vanished all at once, revealing the lay of the land at last.

All kinds of areas were visible on the various screens. There were also helpful map markings in the lower left of each screen that showed where each camera was located on the game map.

"So *that's* what it looks like!"

"I'm seein' a lot of weird terrain."

In previous Squad Jams, all of these environments would have been visible right from the start, but only now could the audience see them in SJ5.

Lighting up the screens now was aerial footage, as though shot by drones hovering at a thousand feet or so.

One screen displayed a large city.

This was the place where M and Anna had started, with one major street and many tall buildings that either stood or littered the ground after the giant explosion. The screen told the audience that it was in the upper right of the map, the northeast quadrant.

Another screen displayed desert wasteland.

It was earthy, full of brown sand, rocks, and rubble. This was where Clarence had started.

That was to the west—or the left—of the city zone, covering nearly two miles of the center of the map. From top to bottom, north to south, it was about a mile and a quarter.

The audience noticed right away how the city abruptly turned into wasteland, across a razor-thin margin.

"What the hell is that?!"

"That's not real map design!"

"They just pasted the regions at right angles!"

"That's lazy programming!"

"Man, that would be so easy... If only you could do that all the time, my life would be so much better..."

"Hey, guys! I found a game designer! He's right here!"

On another screen was a space crossed with many sets of rails, eating into the wasteland. This was the switchyard.

As seen before in SJ3, a switchyard was a place with many parallel rails, where freight cars could be moved, exchanged, and parked. This one was a scaled-down version of the previous, about a mile across.

The switchyard was where Fukaziroh had started, and in this case, it was arranged diagonally from the upper right to the lower left. At its end, the tracks narrowed to just a few, which continued out beyond the edge of the game map.

On another screen was the northwest part of the map. Above and to the left of the switchyard was a mountain.

This was where MMTM's leader had started. Its exterior was all white rock and green grass. There were no trees there.

Several peaks ran along the mountain's length, jagged as the teeth of a saw. The white boulders littering this area were about the size of houses.

On another screen was a highway.

It was quite wide and very sturdily built. This road started out of a tunnel coming from the mountainous zone in the northwest part of the map. It looked like you could get inside the tunnel, but the other exit was unlikely to be anywhere within the map.

The highway went directly south in a straight line into the southwest part of the map. The only thing to either side of the highway was flat black earth.

Though the crowd watching in the pub couldn't have known, the highway was where Llenn had started. It was where she had met Vivi and had nearly got hit by the car.

The bodies were gone by now, but the flipped-over Outback Wilderness still remained.

On another screen was a residential area.

Big, fancy houses lined the streets, all of them abandoned and falling apart, with a huge black blast zone in the center. The closer to the blast zone, the less remained of the houses.

"What's with that huge explosion mark? Was that always there?" asked one of the audience members.

"That's certainly possible, but on the other hand, just maybe…," someone else murmured.

"The bomb team!" several people chimed in at once.

Naturally, the audience was suspicious.

"DOOM, right? But that name isn't on the list."

"They can hide it by simply registering under a different name. That's what I'd do."

"Did anyone fight them in the preliminary round?"

People called around the bar, but no one came forward to admit it.

They didn't know who fought them, and they couldn't have known.

In fact, the frequently participating team that fought DOOM—in this case, BOKR—during the preliminary round so underestimated their opponent that they got entirely eliminated in a single blast and were too embarrassed to show up at the bar today.

On the adjacent screen to the one showing the residential neighborhood was a forest. It was a place of massive trees that took over the middle of the southern part of the map. It was entirely green, connecting the neighboring residential area and snowfield.

"That's so simple… If I could get away with that, it would be sooo easy to design maps…"

"Check it out. The game designer's still here!"

The snowy field was a flat white desert.

It looked like it could be Antarctica. In order to fit this zone, which took up the entire lower right quarter of the map, the camera had to be pulled up to a considerable altitude. There was no way to know who was down there.

The screens in the pub displayed almost all the different zones of the game—except for one.

"They haven't shown the center yet."

As someone just said, the middle of the map.

The center, the core of the map, which measured six miles to a side in its entirety.

And it contained...

"What is that?"

"Ummm, a castle?"

"Yeah, that's a castle."

A castle.

It was a European-style castle surrounded by a circular wall with a diameter of a mile and three-quarters.

The stone wall was a hundred feet tall, with a large rampart about seventy feet wide. It was almost like an elevated highway.

Parapets jutted outward here and there, either to prevent falls or for defensive purposes, with the occasional embrasure: window slots to shoot through with a gun.

Naturally, there was a gate. No one would be able to get in otherwise.

There was actually more than one gate. In fact, every thousand feet there was a very large opening in the wall about 150 feet wide and 30 feet tall.

By rough calculation, the circumference of the wall was a bit less than six miles, which meant there were very many gates, in fact. At least thirty-three of them, going again by rough calculation.

It was like a castle wall decayed with cavities. If a wall was meant to serve a defensive purpose, this one was an utter failure of design. Who built this? Show yourself!

And none of the gates actually had, well, a gate. Every one of them offered free access. There were no signs to be seen, so it would seem that it didn't even cost for admittance.

Since the cameras were aerial, there was a very clear view of the inside of the castle. Right inside the gates was a flat interior space for about five hundred yards. The circular castle was in the middle, so the yard was perfectly donut shaped.

There were many stone buildings placed within that yard. It

looked like a town at first glance, but it was probably not for that purpose—more like a selection of places for players to hide.

The center of the donut was the castle keep itself.

It was a massive circular castle, a whole mile and a quarter in diameter.

If there was a castle that size in the real world, it would have bankrupted the entire country to build it.

The foundation wall was like a cliff, looming 160 feet tall, with spires placed at equal intervals around the edge, eight in total.

Those towers were another 160 feet tall. Each one was the height and size of a high-rise building.

The central room of the castle was a vast, round chamber measuring nearly a mile across. It was like a coliseum of sorts, with all kinds of cover objects placed around the room.

There was a bridge over to the castle itself. It was a stone arch bridge that rose slightly. It was a hundred feet wide and a stunning five hundred yards long.

If you wanted to build a bridge like this in the real world, you couldn't make it out of stone. You might not be able to make it out of anything else, either.

The European-style castle was reminiscent of the castle where Llenn and her friends had done the playtest, but this one was several times larger and taller.

"What a huge freakin' castle, man. But…"

"Yeah. Even knowing there's such a massive building there now…"

The audience had figured it out. They noticed right away.

"…nobody's going to go in there. It's too hard to fight in."

That was correct.

An unnatural environment that was built like a theme park attraction was actually harder to fight in. Anyone familiar with the common sense of *GGO* would not run for shelter inside that castle.

So normally, you would expect that no combat would occur there.

But the castle had been placed there.

"Which means…"

"Yeah."

The audience had figured it out.

One man swirling a wineglass in his hand spoke for the rest of the group.

"It's going to be a setup. There's going to be some scenario that forces you to go there."

Clarence and Tanya were on a lookout platform near the very top floor of the stone tower when it happened.

They saw the mist below clear instantly, revealing the bottom of their tower, the large castle, the even larger courtyard, and the castle walls that surrounded them. It helped that they were at a height of three hundred feet.

A notice appeared informing them of their ammo returning, but they ignored it for more pressing matters.

"We gotta hurry!" Tanya said.

"Sure do," agreed Clarence, waving her left hand to bring up a window, then touched the button for her comm. She attempted to connect to the teammates registered on it. According to the extra rules at the start of the game, you would be able to reconnect with any registered teammate, no matter how far apart you were.

Three seconds later, she contacted her teammates from the start of the game.

Now Clarence and Tanya had the ability to share information directly with all their teammates.

So before she even said hello, Tanya shouted, "Everybody! Hurry to the middle of the map now! There's a castle here, and you can get right inside with all the gates! If you don't, you'll die! Everywhere else, where you guys are, is gonna crumble and fall away!"

With a gleeful grin, Clarence told her distant teammates, "Heya, Llenn and everyone else! Listen! Your areas are all gonna crumble away eventually, and it'll only leave the castle left. They wrote the special rule on the castle walls. Isn't that messed up? Ha-ha-ha! I'm fine because I'm already inside the castle. So don't worry. The team won't be totally wiped out! Well—good luck!"

The audience in the pub saw it at the same moment that the pair were informing all their teammates.

On one of the screens was the wall around the castle in the center of the map. It was a close-up.

Now they could see the writing on the wall, which wasn't visible from the aerial angles. It was a message written plainly in a generic Mincho font.

This land will eventually fall into ruin, and when it is done, only what is within these walls will remain. All who still live, enter now while you can. Make it your final sanctuary. If you have seen this message, spread it to your distant companions when your ability to do so is restored.

That was the very same message that Tanya and Clarence had read when they arrived at the wall earlier. It was written all over the walls. In fact, it was designed so that the letters would appear when any player reached within a certain distance.

The audience understood its meaning, but they had a question, too.

"Why is it in Mincho?"

"How should I know?!"

That aside, someone else had a more direct question.

"What does it mean by, 'the land will fall into ruin'?"

That's a very good question, and here's the answer! the screen seemed to say, because that very moment, all the monitors in the bar switched to the exact same image. It was like someone had messed with the channel at the wall of TVs in an electronics shop.

It was an aerial angle showing the entire field map of SJ5 from above, like a map screen. And it kept zooming out, pulling back.

The camera-carrying drone almost seemed like it was losing control and floating out into space, but the audience quickly understood that it was showing them this for a particular purpose.

They realized what they were seeing and what they were meant to see.

"Whoa!"

"What the hell?!"

"Yikes!"

The outer edge of the map itself was a cliff.

Beyond the boundary of the SJ5 map, the ground simply vanished into empty air. The sheer cliff gave way to an intimidating downward drop, with only flat, brown earth below.

Based on the size of the arena itself, at six miles to a side, the cliff had to be nearly two miles tall.

In other words, the map of SJ5 was basically located on top of a flat, square mountain, at an altitude of ten thousand feet. No wonder it had been covered in fog.

A massive, table-like surface jutting up out of the ground.

"It's just like a tabletop mountain," one of the audience members said. He was correct. A tabletop mountain was a mountain with a flat top. The *tepuis* found in Guyana were a good example.

SJ5's fog-shrouded field was on top of a very, very tall cliff. Nobody had noticed because the mist made it impossible to see.

If they had run at full speed in that direction without knowing, they would have fallen right off a ten-thousand-foot cliff and died. A terrifying way to limit the edges of your map.

A number of screens switched away from the full-map view.

One displayed a highway that ended in midair.

Another displayed a snowfield that ended in midair.

Yet another displayed a mountain that ended…

A forest...

A wasteland...

And all those cliffs began to crumble.

"Huh? What? No way!"

There was one player within SJ5 who saw this collapse happen before anyone else and closer than anyone else.

It was Tomtom, the member of ZEMAL who had been placed in the leader position this time. His trademarks were his ripped body and the bandana he wrapped around his head.

He wore a green fleece jacket, the uniform of ZEMAL, with the backpack-style ammo-loading system behind him and a sweet FN MAG machine gun.

In this case, Mr. Nice Guy was in the lower right, the very southeastern tip of the map.

He'd started SJ5 on the snowfield, and following Vivi's instructions to stay within his means and focus on survival, he chose to make his stand right in the corner.

Earlier, Fukaziroh and Llenn had been talking about this very subject.

"Oh, I know what's going on here. Since he's at the edge of the map, the enemy can only come from ahead of him. So he can keep shooting without worrying about his back."

"Ah, I see... And whatever dark shapes he sees ahead of him, he can shoot without fear."

As it turned out, they were exactly correct.

Tomtom had set up in what he believed was likely the very edge of the battle map, waited for the foes who would see his dot on the Satellite Scan and come rushing toward him, and used his overwhelming machine-gun firepower to destroy them.

He had obliterated five foes so far, mostly during the early stages.

Is that it? I was hoping for more. I'm getting bored, he thought. Of course, he had no idea that Shirley, zipping around the snow on her skis, was eliminating most of the targets before they could get to him.

When the clock hit two PM and Tomtom could see without any fog at all, he thought about moving his position.

But then, from about ten yards behind him, he noticed an ominous sound and spun around.

Rrrmmbmbbrattlerattlerattle.

But there was already nothing left when he turned to see.

"Huh? Oh, no way!"

Even as the words escaped his mouth, the ground was already vanishing beneath his feet.

The earth that composed the tabletop mountain, and the tightly packed snow surface on top of it, crumbled.

"Noooooooooooooooooooooo!"

And with them, they took Tomtom, who plummeted ten thousand feet.

He didn't even have time to hook up his comm to his teammates again.

"Jake! Anyone else who's near the edge of the map! Get away from there right now! This place is going to crumble real soon and leave nothing but the center behind! Everyone, get to the castle in the center as fast as you can!"

It was 2:00:30.

The one giving orders was David, the not-current-leader of MMTM.

It was the first thing he yelled as soon as he'd connected his comm to his teammates' once again.

He was not actually inside the castle, but he could see its walls at the moment. In fact, he was at the edge of the switchyard, hiding out among the abundance of freight cars.

It was the same thing that Pitohui had done in SJ3. In other words, he'd slipped inside a car tough enough to block bullets, then used a lightsword to create a tiny hole that he could see through. After that, he'd just waited for time to pass.

After breaking off from the group with Llenn, David chose this tactic and survived the rest of the way without firing a shot or being shot at in return.

When the mist cleared earlier, he could see the castle in the distance. After peering at it through the scope, he was able to make out large Mincho font letters on the castle wall.

"What...the...?"

His spine trembled as he read the message. There was only one thing he could yell into the comm now that it was working again.

That nasty, mean-spirited sponsor had laid another trap for them.

A team that had chosen to shelter in place from the start of the game and never made any moves was never going to see this information written on the castle wall.

So the trap was going to collapse beneath the feet of those who had no idea what was happening, right as they got knocked out of SJ5.

David just happened to see the message because he was hiding in the switchyard. It was a total coincidence. If he had been hiding in that brick house until two o'clock, he'd probably have been too far away to see the message.

Jake, who had the leader mark on the map, was hiding out in the northwest part of the arena. He was in the most danger. And there were other teammates out there somewhere who hadn't died yet, either.

"Got that?! The center! Hurry! If you run across any enemies, try to let them know, and avoid combat!"

"Everyone, listen closely. This place is going to crumble starting from the outside. Head toward the castle in the middle of the map."

In a spacious train car, another player was doing the exact same thing, alerting their teammates to the impending danger.

It was Vivi.

She had been working with David and was, in fact, in the same car.

In the upper left corner of her vision, the list of her teammates now displayed an X next to Tomtom's name. He was the second death, after Shinohara.

It was very easy to guess that he'd died as a result of the terrain collapse. The leader mark transferred down the line to Peter.

ZEMAL now had four members remaining.

"Let's all meet up at the castle. Don't die."

"Hyeow! That cliff is collapsing *fast*!"

"Yeah! Break it down! Crumble to bits!"

The audience in the pub was alive again, working off the frustration of the last hour's boredom.

On screens all over the room, the terrain was collapsing rapidly.

The vertical cliffs were crumbling away in a fascinating manner. It was the kind of grandiose destruction that just couldn't happen in real life.

They could also see the people dying as a result of the collapse. Tomtom was one of them, falling right off the edge of the snowfield.

The collapse of the city, where Anna and M had started, was quite spectacular. As the ground gave way, the towering buildings tilted and fell, breaking apart in the process.

There was a player running desperately down the street who had been hiding in a building near the edge of the map up to this point. But no matter how hard he ran, the speed of the crumbling was faster, and he soon tumbled away along with the cracked road beneath his feet.

"At this rate, it'll only be a few minutes before everything aside from the castle has fallen away," someone muttered.

The others couldn't know if that estimation was correct, but they decided it was, because that would be more entertaining.

"Yes, it would be fun if it were that fast."

"If they don't make it in time, they deserve to die."

It's always fun to watch dynamic, tremendous spectacles play out from a safe and cozy location.

"I know it's too late now, but I wish I was there, too...," someone muttered, with a glass in his hand.

"I get it. I wish I was in the castle, picking off the people who are trying to run to safety," someone replied.

The man with the glass said, "No, not that. I...I want to fall. You only get to do that once in your life, so the only option for me is to do it in a game instead. But no other games will let you fall from such a tall height..."

"Oh...yeah..."

No one else spoke to him after that.

Here and there on the map, the players who were already in the castle, or were close enough to understand the situation, were panicking. Panicking and rushing toward the castle keep in the center.

Those unlucky enough to have failed to learn the truth came wandering out when the mist disappeared and made for good targets. Many of them got shot.

"Hey, people! Is that really the top priority right—? *Gahk!*"

"Don't shoot, you idiot! We gotta head for the cast— *Grfh!*"

"Just hear me out, okay?! Stop this and run for— *Daah!*"

Sadly, many more players found themselves knocked out of the game.

Meanwhile, having received the news from Clarence, Pitohui was delighted.

"Ah-ha-ha! What a messed-up idea! It's the return of the cruise ship from SJ3! Wah-ha-ha-ha! Oh, that takes me back!"

She was very delighted, indeed. In SJ3, the island on which the players were fighting was sinking. The waterline had been rising bit by bit ever since the beginning of the game, forcing the players steadily toward the luxury cruise liner hidden in the center of the map.

Of course, on top of that there had also been the insane rule that each team had a single member who was secretly chosen to be a betrayer.

Llenn was aghast. "This is not a laughing matter at all, Pito. C'mon, let's hurry!"

But no sooner had she said that than Fukaziroh said, "Wait, hold on. Just a bit longer. If you go now…"

The sound of abrupt fighting broke out through the woods.

"…you're going to get stuck in a stupid and pointless fight between the people who know what's going on and the people who don't. Just hold off for a minute or two."

"Hrmph…" Llenn had no choice but to take her advice.

At her side, Boss said, "Good job, Tanya. Protect yourself with Clarence."

Tanya had provided them with the crucial information they needed. To the others, she announced, "Hey, girls! Did you all hear that? Let's meet up at the castle! I'm going to head there from the forest to the south, along with Llenn, Fuka, and Pitohui!"

Though Llenn couldn't hear it, she seemed to be getting the other girls' responses. According to Boss, no one in SHINC had died yet.

The four of them then heard a different voice.

"You're in the forest? That's fantastic," said M.

"The two of us will go to join you! Where are you?" asked Anna. It seemed that M had patched Anna into the group's channel.

"Wow, it's M! And Anna! You're close! Come on over! We're at…um…"

Llenn tried to figure out how to describe their location and came up short.

"It's about five-seven," said Pitohui. She was quoting the style of shogi notation where the first number referred to the columns, starting from the right, and the second number referred to the rows, starting from the top.

"Got it. We'll be there in one minute from the west. Watch the perimeter for us."

In less than a minute, Llenn's group greeted M and Anna.

Yes! she cheered to herself. Now they had a party of six. That was very reassuring.

"We can celebrate our reunion later. Let's go to the castle," M said without a hint of pleasure. He was busy taking his shield out of his backpack.

He combined them vertically in two parts. One he kept for himself.

"Here you go."

"Thanks."

And the other he gave to Pitohui.

They didn't even need to speak to know what the other was thinking. The two of them would stand at the lead, and if anyone was out there trying to shoot at the group, they'd hold up their shields to block the shots.

Equally silent, Fukaziroh and Boss assumed the rear position, with Llenn and Anna comprising the center of the formation.

"Let's go."

They couldn't see the crumbling of the earth yet, but they couldn't stay here forever.

The three pairs of the group took an interval of about ten yards each and began to move toward the large castle visible in the distance.

With each stretch of ground, the trees in front thinned out, so the castle was quite clear from here. They had probably two-thirds of a mile to go.

When she looked over her shoulder, she still saw only woods, so the collapse wasn't rushing up on them yet, Llenn wanted to believe. She had no other choice.

It would've been nice if the device map would show them how much of the land had fallen away, but of course, the piece of crap writer wouldn't allow for that.

Tat-tat-tat-tat-dat-tam! Gunfire broke out.

Ga-gank-gang-ting! M's shield deflected the bullets.

"Enemy ahead on the right!" M announced.

Llenn dropped to the ground at once, so she didn't see the enemy. But it was clear that someone who was ignorant of the situation was firing at them.

"Ugh, honestly!" Pitohui fumed. She stuck her shield into the ground for support, then returned fire with a fierce burst from the KTR-09 assault rifle.

Automatic fire after automatic fire. She sprayed bullets for several seconds, more than willing to empty her entire seventy-five-round drum. The gun only stopped firing after Llenn started wondering if she was maybe going a bit overboard.

"Got 'em," M muttered.

The two in the lead resumed moving forward, as though the interruption had not happened at all.

Llenn got back to her feet and continued walking, watching the right side for movement. About fifty yards away in the distance, she saw a DEAD tag.

"Huh?"

In fact, there were two. A pair of players had died and fallen on top of each other in the same spot.

In other words, the strategy was that if the first player was shot and killed, the person behind them would continue shooting— perhaps making use of the body as an impenetrable shield.

But Pitohui had figured them out instantly and hit them with a merciless stream of automatic gunfire. It wasn't just an overkill situation, where she was taking it out pointlessly on a dead player. She had a reason for what she did.

"She's very good," Boss commented.

You said it, Llenn thought.

Carefully, she continued her watch as they followed the lead pair. Eventually, the forest came to an end. Beyond the last of the massive trees, the castle was clear and unmissable. The group came to a stop next to a nearby tree.

Although the castle was visible now, there were about five hundred yards of space left, treeless and empty, with no feature beyond dry brown earth.

M created cover for himself with the tree trunk and his shield, then used binoculars to examine the castle wall.

"They're up there. Quite a few, atop the walls straight ahead. Seems like they want to snipe anyone rushing up to the gates."

Campers! Llenn fumed to herself.

"Campers!" Fukaziroh fumed out loud. She added, "If we were a bit closer, I'd be feeding my grenade launchers fresh blood."

Her MGL-140 launchers had a maximum range of four hundred yards. Even adding the sixty-foot diameter of her plasma grenades, they weren't going to cover five hundred yards. It was out of range.

"If not for the collapse behind us, we could gain ground with sniper support," Boss said bitterly.

This made sense to Llenn. Five hundred yards was certainly a manageable distance for a sniper to aim at a human target. And they could offer support from the woods by either sniping the attackers or at least getting them to stay down and out of sight so the others could rush toward the castle.

M and Anna would hang back by the trees to offer support while the others moved forward, and when she was within effective range, Fukaziroh could help with her sheer firepower. Once they were safely at the castle, they would call M and Anna to join them—the most standard of tactical moves. This would probably work, except that M and Anna might get left behind when the collapse reached them. It had a much higher chance of causing two to die, but *only* two.

"All right!" Pitohui said brightly.

"Oh? You got a brilliant plan for us?" Llenn asked with great optimism.

"I do! M and Anna will have to die here."

"Hold on."

I was a fool for expecting anything better, Llenn thought.

"But, I mean, isn't that the best option? M and Anna have taken the most damage in combat so far, too."

"I know, but—!"

"Should we all rush the castle and get shot?"

"I don't want that, either, but..."

"And we're wasting time just sitting around worrying about it."

"But..."

Llenn had run out of rebuttals.

"Let's do it, M."

"Sure."

With just those two short messages, the pair of Pitohui and M performed their gear-switch.

M's M14 EBR vanished, as did his defensive shield, replaced by a monster the same weight as both of them: the six-foot-plus Alligator antimateriel rifle. This would enable him to do even more devastating sniping.

Pitohui's KTR-09 assault rifle disappeared, too, along with her Remington M870 Breacher. Instead, she had a machine gun now.

This was the collection piece Pitohui had deigned to bring along this time: a general-purpose machine gun that used 7.62 mm rounds, the H&K MG5.

The rugged exterior was colored brown. The stock could be retracted or folded, it featured a rounded optical sight, and it was a newer gun in both *GGO* and the real world. If any of the ZEMAL crowd were here, their eyes would be sparkling right now.

It had a box attached to the left side of the gun containing a 120-round belt link of ammo. Pitohui loaded the first shot into the gun.

"All right, let's move! Say good-bye to those two, everyone," she said heartlessly.

"Don't worry. If we can catch up, we will." M beamed, accepting the possibility of his own death.

Anna said, "Leave the backup to us!" her voice bright, despite the fact that her sunglasses could have been hiding tears.

"Awww..." Llenn felt quite upset about this, but if M and Anna had made up their minds, she couldn't protest. There was no time for lengthy farewells.

"Okay, start in ten seconds," M said, placing the giant Alligator on a bipod and lying down behind it. He operated the large bolt handle, sending its first huge bullet into the firing chamber.

"Best of luck, everyone!" said Anna, pressing herself against a tree with her Dragunov in hand. This would stabilize her aim.

"Five, four, three," Fukaziroh counted down with anticipation.

But just as she was saying *two*, Pitohui snapped, "Wait!"

Llenn had just been mentally preparing herself to rush into the lead, as the smallest and quickest target, distracting the enemies with her presence.

"Eep!" she yelped, P90 quivering. "What is it?" she asked Pitohui.

"Something weird's coming. On the right."

"Huh?"

Llenn looked over to the right, as Pitohui had indicated.

Everyone saw it then.

A vehicle approaching from their right.

It had two skis in front, with a track in the rear, or perhaps a caterpillar tread: a snowmobile.

The body was a faded yellow color. While it was quite far away still, it was clear from here that there was only one person riding in it. The snowmobile was designed for smooth and easy riding over snow, but if you wanted to, you could use it to cross flat earth as well.

But you had to be careful about running it for too long, because the engine might overheat. The radiator was over the track, so when running over snow, the track would lift the snow up to hit and cool the radiator. (Whether *GGO* implemented this level of mechanical physics was unknown.)

This vehicle had clearly come from the snowfield zone, and it was now racing straight for the castle. It was quite fast.

Peering through her rifle scope, Anna called out, "It's the suicide bombers!"

Whut? Everyone used whatever items they had to get a closer look.

Llenn pulled out her monocular and saw for herself. She didn't even want to look at those guys. The ones with armor over their bodies and on top of the huge backpacks they wore. She'd seen one earlier, and it had disastrous consequences. She'd been through hell.

"Lemme see?" asked Fukaziroh, leaning closer, so she put the monocular to her friend's eye.

"Is he gonna get into the castle before he blows up?" wondered Boss, peering through the Vintorez's scope.

"No…I don't think that'll work. The castle itself should be indestructible, unlike the ship in SJ3," M replied calmly.

"That's good," said Llenn, the very person who ultimately destroyed that ship.

"Exactly. Otherwise, we'll lose the place where we're supposed to be running for shelter," agreed Fukaziroh, following gamer logic.

Yes, that makes sense. It would have to work that way, Llenn understood. If that man and his teammates could blow up the castle, it would basically mean the premature end of the game.

If the castle were to be destroyed while there were still players left, and they were unable to attack one another, SJ5 would never end, unless someone got fed up with it and either committed suicide or resigned.

But that did leave the mystery behind of what would happen with all the explosive force and blast wind pressure.

That aside, M lifted the Alligator and said, "This is a good opportunity for us. Use him as a decoy or his blast as cover for all of us to charge up."

Llenn thought he might go back to his M14 EBR, but he did not. He wasn't giving up on providing support if it was necessary.

The snowmobile drew closer to the castle. It was driving up a great trail of dust, which drew attention. People were shooting from the castle ramparts. The lines of fire moved twice as fast as the sound, stabbing at the DOOM member.

But the bullets bounced off harmlessly. At a distance of four hundred yards, they weren't able to puncture his armor.

The shooting from the castle grew even fiercer.

They must have noticed that it was DOOM. Everyone who was up there, most likely from a variety of teams, started shooting at the greatest threat at the moment. Probably everyone who could see him had joined in by now.

But the snowmobile didn't slow down.

"That's it! Go, go, go!" cheered Fukaziroh, lifting her MGL-140s in exultation.

You know that if you make too much noise, they'll snipe you from the castle, Llenn thought scornfully about her partner.

Two hundred yards left until the castle. Suddenly, the snowmobile began to slow down—and just like that, it stopped.

"Aaah!" Llenn exclaimed.

"The engine in the front got knocked out. The track works on a lot of friction, so it can't keep sliding along out of inertia," M explained.

"What's he going to do?" Boss asked.

"Maybe run from there?" Fukaziroh said.

"Or maybe…," Anna wondered.

The answer: He exploded.

In the bar, the screens were engulfed in the glow of an orange ball of light and the white sphere of the shock wave that grew from it.

Then there was a colossal noise that threatened to destroy the speakers throughout the room.

"Whoaaaaaa!"

"He did it!"

"Fireworks!"

"Way to go!"

"That's our DOOM!"

"Since when were they yours?"

The crowd erupted into cheers and comments. There had been running commentary ever since the snowmobile appeared on-screen, and the camera followed his glorious dash from just over the shoulder.

They had groaned and lamented when the engine got shot, prematurely ending his mad dash for the castle gates. But the explosion brought them roaring to their feet again.

They were having quite a time.

"This is our chance! Don't let the blast stop you! Prepare!" M said as the shock wave swallowed up his words.

The explosion happened over three hundred yards away, but even still, the force of it punched them hard. The trees were being whipped back and forth.

The group stayed flat on the ground, waiting out the seconds until the violent force of the initial shock wave passed.

"Waaagh!" Llenn was so light, she nearly got blown away.

"Yo!" Boss's thick arm reached over to hold her down.

"Thanks!"

Once the first wave had safely passed, M called out, "Now go! Just run straight there!"

The group got to their feet and began to run through the sudden dust screen that covered the world before their eyes.

As he expected, there was dust everywhere in the air now. There was no longer any worry about the players at the castle being able to see them. There was just one other problem.

"How long do you think this will hold up?" Llenn asked as she ran. No one was able to give an answer.

The wind died down, and then the air began to rush backward to fill the vacuum. It roared from left back to right.

Llenn could not see her teammates through the dust; she could only keep running until the moment she smacked into the castle wall. If she got close enough, they wouldn't be able to shoot down at her from the ramparts, and more importantly, she could get inside.

Of course, there would be other enemies in there, too. But she could worry about that when they got there. Right now, she was going to die if she didn't get into the castle.

Naturally, there were no shots at them from the walls. No one could see them.

"Tanya, Clarence," said M, "we're heading for the castle, hiding in the dust from the explosion to the south."

Clarence's response came in her usual lackadaisical tone. "Okay, cool. Wow, what an explosion. I'm sure you don't want to hear this, but the collapse is getting pretty close. Don't slow down now."

"Got it."

Llenn ran, ran, and ran for all she was worth.

"Hyeep!"

Until she almost ran through the dust smack into the wall itself.

She had to slam on the metaphorical brakes and twisted around until she finally stopped by smashing back-first into the bricks.

"I reached the wall!"

"If there's a gate, wait there."

"Got it!"

Llenn started walking along the wall, tracing it with her free hand, with the dust cloud around her. She had seen a gate when looking straight at the castle earlier, but now that she was right next to the wall, she couldn't tell which direction the gate was in.

Should I go right? How long do I have to walk? she wondered. Suddenly, she was touching nothing but air.

Here was the castle gate. The entrance to her salvation.

"Found it! I was going straight to the wall, and then it was on my right!"

"Wait there. When you see someone else arrive, call them over."

"Got it!"

M was referring to their teammates, Llenn understood. They ought to regroup at the gate, then go inside the castle grounds as a team.

Several seconds later, Boss was the next to arrive. She spotted Llenn through the cloud of dust.

"Hey."

She took position next to Llenn and kept her gun pointed into the castle grounds.

They couldn't see more than thirty feet through the cloud. There was no way to know what was happening on the other side.

Eventually, Fukaziroh showed up, followed by Anna. Fukaziroh took position behind Llenn, and Anna stuck next to Boss.

The only ones left were Pitohui and M.

I think we're all going to make it, thanks to that explosion! Llenn hoped. Right then, M came through the dust. His Alligator was literally held in his hands like a spear. He probably could have killed her with it if he'd run into her.

To this point, still no one had shot at the group.

"Hey, gang, thanks for waiting!"

Pitohui came last. At first Llenn was momentarily alarmed, because the MG5 machine gun was such an unfamiliar sight on her, but it was indeed Pitohui.

And right as they all regrouped, the wind blew.

Whether it was some final blowback from the explosion or a helpful gale sent by the game system to blow away the dust, a stronger-than-usual wind picked up and cleared out the cloud that had been hanging around them.

The sky returned from cloudy brown to its usual reddened blue, revealing what was beyond the castle gate.

"Be on the lookout!" M instructed, holding his Alligator at the waist. All the others pointed their guns into castle.

It was a very spacious courtyard, so the chances of someone being nearby was low, but they were going to be ready to shoot the instant they saw anyone, regardless.

Pitohui came next to Llenn to join the lineup. "Let's get in there and raise some hell."

"It's good to have you on our side, Pito."

"And I'm reassured to have *you* on our side, Llenn."

Friendship between women was blooming on the battlefield.

And it was at that very moment that Llenn saw a bullet damage effect appear on Pitohui's head, along with the white smoke of something exploding.

"Oh?" murmured Pitohui, and then all was quiet.

The damage sparkled, creating an effect that looked like a red head on top of a dark-blue body.

But in fact, it was clear that she was already dead. Pitohui's body toppled toward Llenn with the machine gun in her hand.

"Pito!" Llenn cried. "Mmgh!" She got squished.

"Huh?"

"Hmm?"

Fukaziroh and Boss turned around and saw Llenn, facedown and squashed on the ground.

Ding! And lying atop her, Pitohui's body, featuring a DEAD tag overhead.

"She got got," M said simply.

It was clear from a glance at Pitohui's red head what had happened.

Taking a hit from a rifle shot to the head did not cause it to turn completely red like this. It was the phenomenon to demonstrate a head being exploded. It would simply be too grotesque to actually blow up the player's head. You could cut it off but not blow it up.

In other words, if this were a real combat situation, Pitohui's body would have no head above its shoulders.

There were only two possible explanations for such a powerful bullet.

One: an antimateriel rifle.

Two: an exploding bullet.

"Huh? Pito?"

Llenn tried to lift the body and MG5, but the weight was too much for her.

"Move it!" said Fukaziroh, kicking the body to free her teammate.

This was not the kind of thing you usually did to a friend's body, but her hands were full of the grenade launchers, so that was the quickest way. Nobody complained about it.

"M, what should we do with the machine gun?"

"We're going to make use of it," said M, waving his left hand and putting the Alligator back into storage. He lifted the MG5 and pulled the backup ammo box off Pitohui's side.

Even with all that, M still had room to carry more weight.

"Whaaat?" Llenn exclaimed with shock.

"It was an exploding round," explained M. "Shirley. She wasn't in the castle yet, I guess."

If Pitohui was right near the entrance to the castle, then naturally the shooter would still have to be outside.

"You don't think...," said Anna. Only she would have picked up on this. "...Shirley was teaming up with the man from DOOM in the snowfield, do you?"

M's cheeks twisted into a smirk. "That's probably it. She sent him toward the castle to blow himself up at this moment. All so she could get a clear shot on Pitohui."

"Most impressive," Fukaziroh remarked.

"Awww! Pito!" Llenn was still having trouble recovering from her friend's death.

Fukaziroh used her petite tush to push Llenn along and put some space between her and her fallen teammate before she could start clinging to Pitohui's body.

"Come on. Keep your wits about you, or you'll be next."

"Ugh..."

Llenn took one more look at Pitohui's body on the ground.

"I'm gonna take out whoever did this!" she threatened.

"So...you're gonna eliminate Shirley?"

"Huh? Uh...yeah! Before we win!"

"Sure. You do that," Fukaziroh murmured, poking Llenn in the back with the end of a grenade launcher. "Let's get moving, people. Stick with me!"

"Huh? Are you taking charge?"

"No, I just always wanted to say that. M, take it away."

M clenched the MG5 and said, "All right. We're going into the castle!"

The clock at this time said 2:06.

"I did it… Thank you, little bomber," muttered Shirley.

There was no longer anyone to hear her. The one member of Team BOKR whom she'd been hooked up to had just blown himself up.

As Anna suspected, Shirley had indeed recruited him for her strategy. When she stumbled across him in the mist and got too close to shoot, she had spoken to him instead. *"Hey, how ya doin'?"*

To his shock, she told him, *"It'd be a waste to blow yourself up here."*

To his shock, she told him, *"I can take you to a place where you'll really shine. Let's work together until then."*

Of course, it was a gamble on Shirley's part as to whether he would actually accept her offer.

But to her shock this time, he replied, *"Wow, really, scary sniper lady? Yeah, I'll follow you! I was just feeling lonely, being separated from my team!"*

Based on his tone of voice, he seemed like he was very young. They spoke more over time, and he shocked her even more by blithely admitting that he was still just in middle school.

So the member of BOKR had more or less become Shirley's follower. He told her the tag was an abbreviation of *Bokura*—in a word, *Us*.

While Shirley was busy taking out the enemies on the snowfield, she had him look around for a vehicle of any kind. Even on a totally flat and featureless plain, they would have hidden something somewhere.

After a painstaking search, he announced that he had found a snowmobile hidden in a hole. It was a large hole with a white board placed over it.

She told him to take it, ride it to the very eastern edge of the field, and wait there.

It was after that point that Shirley helped out M and Anna. After saving them and seeing them off, it was two o'clock before you knew it.

"Uh-oh, Miss Shirley! We gotta get to the castle quick!" he told her, which was how she learned what was happening. She called him back at once, and they rode the snowmobile together to the edge of the snowfield closest to the castle.

At that point, she didn't know whether Llenn and Pitohui were still in the forest or if they'd already reached the castle. So she had to take the option that guaranteed her own survival: rushing the castle.

But now that the mist had cleared, moving across a nearly five-hundred-yard empty space in full view was dangerous. If she got closer, the people already in the castle would be able to gang up on her—even if she was speeding on a snowmobile.

While she was deliberating, her new friend, the little bomber, said, "I'll blow myself up part of the way, and that'll create a dust cloud that'll be your smoke screen. Then you can use that to get into the castle!"

After a bit more thinking, Shirley gave her order:

"Clear the way for me to do my thing."

"With pleasure, ma'am!"

Then the explosion.

And the dust cloud.

Shirley started running straight for the castle wall.

And right at that moment, someone started to whisper into her mind.

"Mai, if you stay here, maybe you'll get the chance to shoot that hateful Pitohui in the head."

Grandma!

It was the voice of her grandmother.

Still alive and well, by the way.

Shirley got down on hands and knees at the border between the snow and dirt and set up the R93 Tactical 2 on a bipod.

She was aiming for the path from the forest to the castle.

If Pitohui's team was still in the forest, then they would've made a move for the castle through the dust cloud.

In which case…

Shirley waited.

Pressed to the ground as she was, she could feel subtle vibrations. They were getting bigger.

She didn't need to turn around to understand. The ground was crumbling behind her.

There was no way for her to know how far behind it was. Perhaps the dirt supporting her body would give way in the very next second, sending her to her doom.

Still, she waited.

And waited.

And waited.

And when the dust cleared and she could see the castle gate through her scope, she murmured, "Gotcha…"

She adjusted her aim just a tiny bit and caught Pitohui right in her sights.

Her target was Pitohui's center of gravity.

The distance was half a mile.

The bullet would drop over time, so she had to aim a full person's height higher.

She wasn't relying on the system to aim for her, so she wouldn't produce a bullet line that gave away her presence. It was a pure snipe shot based on nothing but player skill.

Even with her incredible talent, this distance was pushing it in terms of Shirley's accuracy.

If she misjudged the bullet's drop even the tiniest bit, the bullet would easily sail over Pitohui's head.

Carefully, slowly, but firmly, Shirley pulled the trigger.

When she lowered the scope after the recoil jump, she could see Pitohui's beet-red head.

Her aim had been off slightly, but only up to her head. It must've been instantly fatal.

"I did it… Thank you, little bomber."

Shirley got to her feet, loaded her next shot, then finally turned around.

The white snowfield turned into sky partway. The boundary was about four hundred yards away.

Then it was 380. In less than twenty seconds, the ground under her was going to crumble, too.

For just an instant, Shirley considered it.

But only for an instant.

"I can't die yet!"

She took off running with the R93 Tactical 2 in hand.

Running for the castle gate before her eyes.

✳   ✳   ✳

"Gaaah! She got me!"

In the dark of the waiting area, Pitohui writhed in frustration, alone.

Her presence there was an instant tip-off that she'd been one-hit-killed.

"I know it was Shirley!"

She hadn't actually seen the shot that hit her, but she was certain: It was Shirley who did it.

Considering the feelings behind the bullet that hit her, the grudge that went into it, she couldn't imagine anyone other than Shirley.

That is, assuming such things were actually real in the virtual world.

"Well, shit."

She flopped onto her back with her limbs splayed out and stared at a countdown clock on the wall with a timer at 9:40.

If she waited here for nine minutes, she'd be back at the pub.

"Guess I could drown my sorrows there," she muttered. But just then, a message appeared in the corner of her field of vision.

It was at the very top of what she could see, staring up at the ceiling, meaning it was on the wall behind her.

"Huh?"

She sat up and turned her head to look at it.

"Huh!"

She took note of what it said.

About the special rules of SJ5: Here are some more! It's very important! Read carefully! Don't give up just because you're dead!

Below that was a very long explanatory text.

Only those who have died in SJ5 get to read this. We have a very special opportunity for all of you!

"Ohhh?" Pitohui murmured. She read further.

You may have died, but there's still something you can do, right? Yes, you can come back and haunt people.

"Uh-huh."

So…would you like to be a ghost?

To be continued…

AFTERWORD AND SPECIAL EMOTIONAL CELEBRATION

(Warning: Spoilers for this volume contained in small measure, so please make sure you have finished the book before you read this.)

Playback of Events Prior to SJ5, Part 3

"Hello, hello! How are you? What's going on tonight?"

"Really? That's what you're asking? It's, like, noon here. You knew that, didn't you?"

"Of course I did, Nathan. Your midday is Japan's midnight. Ahhh, that middle-of-the-night ramen here is super-*oishii*-yummy! I can feel it in my soul!"

"I know I ask this every time we talk in English, but seriously, where did you learn your English? Mars? Is that an extraterrestrial accent?"

"Well, in my brain I'm first converting my Japanese into French, then a quick sojourn through German into Russian, and lastly translated to English."

"I'm not childish enough to believe that. I've been through high school, you know."

"Anyway, ignoring all that, is it okay to talk? You aren't too busy?"

"Yes, it's fine. Just get to the point…not that I don't know what it is already."

"Well then, you know what I mean!"

"Say it!"

"But you know, don't you? Yes, please set up the fifth Squad Jam, please and thank you berry-berry much! Go!"

"What language are you speaking...? So it's time for SJ5 already? It seems so fast. Didn't you just do SJ4 at the end of last month and the Five Ordeals this month?"

"True. But have you ever heard the phrase 'Do good deeds when the doing's good'?"

"When is it?"

"September 19th, starting at one PM, Japan Time. Prelims the day before. How's that?"

"Well, we don't have any major maintenance scheduled then, so the date works for us. We'll take the usual cost at a minimum, and knowing you, there's probably some weird rules or bizarre set piece for the map, right? That's gonna bump up the price of putting on the event."

"No problem!"

"Okay, then."

"My recent book, *A Forty-Something Office Worker Gets Reincarnated into an Isekai Identical to Our World, Where She Goes to an All-Girls High School and Accidentally Joins the Kendo Club Rather Than the Chorus Club, Beats All the Boys, and Becomes a Star, Creating Her Own Harem*, is selling a lot better than anyone thought, so I'm pouring my royalties into this event! We're pushing the budget twice as hard!"

"What the hell kind of story is that? Anyway, can we not wait until October? The costs of putting on the event will be a lot more reasonable if you give us more leeway on the schedule."

"No! Absolutely not!"

"Listen, man... Why are you in such a rush these days?"

"N-n-n-n-no reason! Wh-wh-why would I b-be in a r-r-rush?"

"You're hiding something, aren't you?"

"Yyyyessss..."

"...Whatever. SJ5 on 9/19, got it. Give me a rough breakdown. What rules are you thinking of this time?"

"So first of all, at the starting point, there's going to be a ton of fog all over the place, so you can't see your enemies at all! And each squad's members will be scattered around the map at random! That's totally gonna piss everyone off, huh? That's so exciting!"

"You really are a piece of shit. Who do you think you are?"

"The GM is God."

"Take it easy with the god complex. What about the map?"

"Frankenstein! S'monster! All stitched together like that! Just take existing maps like forest and snowfield and city, and just cut them out along right angles and paste them together! Super easy!"

"Well...sure, that's easy...but the players won't be happy."

"So what? Squad Jam players are made of tougher stuff than that. Besides, they love complaining. But then—! The big idea comes at the end! The whole map's gonna be on the top of a flat mountain ten thousand feet tall! Basically, in the geological upheaval after the apocalyptic war, all kinds of terrain got fused together and then pushed upward! It's a perfectly nonsensical and impossible concept!"

"Hey, that's what I was thinking! Anyway, there's no issue putting the map at a height like that, but we don't have any ballistic data for highlands at an altitude of ten thousand feet, so we'll just have to use our sea-level ballistic model, okay? Any loony who shoots enough real guns might be able to tell. Is that cool with you?"

"No protein!"

"Whatever."

"But then, when the time comes, the map will start to crumble! And then..."

"Sure, just e-mail us the details. Don't make me jot all this down. And between you and me, it's impossible to execute all the fine details of what you come up with. Just give us a broad outline instead."

"Yes, sirrity-sir! Also, just this one time, I'm gonna compete again! I'll have my beloved SG 550 in hand!"

"You know, I've always thought, isn't it kind of cheating to have one player in the game who already knows all the secrets and special rules ahead of time?"

"Call it a professional privilege. If I had a nickel for every time I've cheated, I'd be rich by now!"

"Yeah, yeah. Anyway, I'll get it set up."

"Thank you! Now, let's talk about the usual special prize."

"Yeah…"

"I'll send over a whole box of those special Japanese snacks you love so much… Er, I mean, packing material. I'll send it to you, ummm, ummm, in a little one-hundred-yen plastic case but with all the cushioning material needed to protect the contents. You can decide whether you want to eat it or throw it away."

"Heh-heh-heh… Much appreciated, as always…"

"Awww, don't mention it… Heh-heh-heh. Just don't get caught with it, okay…?"

"Don't worry, my man. I'm a pro when it comes to that."

"A pro at what, secretly eating snacks? Must be hard to work at your company. What kind of place has workplace rules against snacking on the job?"

"Unbelievable, right? Crazy, right? It's because the boss is a total health freak… He acts like oil, sugar, and salt killed his parents."

"But that's no reason to forbid your employees from having them. It's mucho bs! Très bs! I bet you could totally sue him and win, huh?"

"Maybe, but do you think it'd be worth the trade-off in terms of crazy lawyer's fees?"

"Nopity-nope."

"What language is that? Anyway, all the employees agree with me."

"What a horribly marginalized community…"

"Okay, now you're getting carried away. Plus, in that 'Japan' place where you live, they put you away for even having a gun, don't they?"

"Oof."

"I got a nine-milli subcompact auto on my hip right now. It's a Glock today, but I feel like I'll be in a SIG mood tomorrow. And maybe a Sturm Ruger the day after that."

"Aaaagh! I'm so jealous! Damn, I'm so jealous! Fakku!"

"Whoa, whoa, that's a word you can't say on TV."

"No, Nathan, it's cool. The word *fakku* is Japanese. It's not like the English F-word. It's a religious Buddhist term, in fact. It means, 'Don't swear!'"

"Huh? Are you serious...?"

"Quite serious. When I almost say a swear word, I shout that word in Japanese instead. Anyway, I'll send over my scenario sheet and those snacks soon!"

At a later date...

"Hey, Nathan! How are you doing?"

"Nathan has been fired. I'm Sophia, and I've taken over his position."

"Um, why?"

"We discovered that he had been eating food that was forbidden by company rules, based on the empty bag in the background of his screen during an online meeting."

"He said he was a pro! Fakku!"

"That language is unacceptable."

"No, you see, it's a Japanese word that means..."

Not to be continued

I once drew these holes
in an in-story illustration
because I thought they
were cool.
But on the approval check, they
said those were used only on
ammo for model guns, and
I had to correct it.
But if it's not for a
real gun, it's okay for
me to draw this
illustration, right?

Kouhaku
Kuroboshi